X-Men

X-Men

A novelization by
Kristine Kathryn Rusch
and
Dean Wesley Smith

Based on the movie
written by
Christopher McQuarrie
and Ed Solomon

A Del Rey® Book
THE BALLANTINE PUBLISHING GROUP • NEW YORK

A Del Rey® Book
Published by The Ballantine Publishing Group
TM and copyright © 2000 by Twentieth Century Fox Film Corporation. All rights reserved.

www.randomhouse.com/delrey/

ISBN 0-345-44346-2

Manufactured in the United States of America

First Edition: June 2000

10 9 8 7 6 5 4 3 2 1

For Keith DeCandido

Acknowledgments

We would like to thank J. Steven York, John Ordover,
Merrilee Heifetz, and Ginger Clark for their help.
And a special thanks to Steve Saffel,
who went far beyond the call of duty.

X-Men

Prolog

Poland—1944

The hard, cold rain pounded out of the sky, soaking clothes, changing the dirt to slippery mud, beating the life out of everyone it touched.

Eric Lehnsherr stood in the mud beside his parents, his coat wet clear through to his shirt, his small hand grasping the back of his father's wool pants just above the knee. His child's eyes were wide at what was happening around him. His mother and father, both strong and sturdy people, held him close, tried to comfort him, shelter him, but the events of that hour were like the rain: impossible to avoid.

The mass of people scared him, making him want to run away. The guards made him want to cry. But he did neither. Instead he focused on the twisting spirals of barbed wire that covered the tops of the fences in front of and around them. Through the rain the points of the wire seemed to sparkle, calling to him.

Suddenly the German guards shoved everyone forward, making them walk between two tall wire fences with more twisting barbed wire lining the top. Eric didn't want to stare at all the faces watching them from the other side of the fences. Those people were all terribly sad and tired, and many were crying as they watched. Some clutched their arms, as if trying to cover the numbers that had been tattooed there.

Instead he traced the curved barbed wire and its shining points as he and his parents continued, slowly moving forward. It was as if that wire were his only friend.

At one point he slipped in the mud, but his father held him up. His mother clutched both him and his father. Together they moved almost as one, following the wet rows of people in front of them, trying to not look at the guards.

Eric told himself he would be strong, for his parents. Strong like the wire.

Ahead of them people were screaming now, and Eric didn't want to get any closer, but his father and the guards moved them along, without saying a word. The people behind them crowded in tight, sometimes bumping him.

A woman behind Eric was crying softly.

The barbed wire on the top of the fence seemed to spin along with them, twisting and sparkling in the hard rain. There had always been something about metal that he loved. The fence and the sharp points of the wire didn't seem dangerous to him. He wished instead that he could climb up there and touch them.

Suddenly, ahead of them, the people moved out of the way, and from where he stood Eric could see that the path turned into two paths, both of which were lined with tall weaved-wire fences. The guards were opening and closing the gates as people went through.

A big guard in a German uniform shoved into them, poking at Eric's mother with a rifle, speaking much too fast for Eric to understand.

His father understood, though, and shook his head. "No." His mother held on to Eric even tighter. So tight it hurt.

The guard poked at them with the rifle and began shouting.

Eric clung to his father, not knowing what was happening.

Then his mother screamed.

"No!" his father said again.

Suddenly two more German guards appeared and yanked Eric away from his parents. With a quick turn they shoved him along after the other children who were being pushed and carried down one of the paths between rows of fences. Many of the children were screaming and shouting and crying. Others were strangely quiet.

The guards then turned their attention to Eric's parents and shoved them down the other path.

Eric started back to them, crying now. He wasn't going to leave them.

He *wasn't*!

They couldn't make him!

But the two guards picked him up and carried him back along the fenced path. Their hands were rough and hurt his skin through his wet coat.

He kicked at them, screamed at them, but they ignored him. They took him through the weaved barbed-wire gate and closed it.

He could still see his parents through the gate, his mother reaching out for him despite the restraint of a guard, screaming his name. His father just stood there, a guard's rifle pointed squarely at his chest.

Eric tried to fight his way back to them, but the guards wouldn't let him down.

He glanced at the fence. A thought flashed across his mind. He needed to be like metal, heavier. He needed to be much heavier, so the guards couldn't carry him anymore!

His feet touched the ground, and he planted them hard in the mud, focused on stopping. He wasn't going anywhere without his parents.

He was going to rip down the fence between them, so they could go with him.

He focused all his anger and fear on the wire gate— and it started to shake.

The guards pulled at him, but now they couldn't move him. He was like the heaviest of metals, too heavy for the guards to budge. They yanked on his arms, hurting him even more, but he didn't care. He wouldn't go with them, not without his mother and father.

He took a step back toward his parents, dragging the guards in the mud with him.

The metal gate twisted and bent in front of him. Some of the strands of barbed wire began breaking, like weak string. Eric knew that gate couldn't stop him.

One guard tried to pick him up and failed, swearing so fast that Eric didn't understand.

All Eric wanted was to tear down the fence and let

his parents come with him. If the Germans wanted him, then his parents would have to come too.

Another guard came up, swearing angrily at the other two.

Eric just focused on the fence, ripping it apart, making it go away. The coiled strands of sparkling barbed wire along the top started to uncurl, whipping about in the air like angry serpents.

The entire compound suddenly got very silent. Only the sound of the rain remained, pounding down in the mud, accented by the snaps of the breaking wire.

More strands broke, and the entire weaved-wire gate bowed toward Eric. It was as if something massive pushed from the other side.

Suddenly the rain stopped hitting Eric as the third guard loomed over him. The other two still were pulling on Eric's arms, futilely, hurting him, making him madder and madder.

And the angrier Eric got, the more the gate and the fences shook and broke apart.

The new guard swore again, then raised his rifle.

Eric could hear his mother's scream cut through the silence and the rain.

His father took a step toward him, wide eyed, only to be stopped.

Then the butt of the guard's rifle came down hard.

For an instant—just an instant—the wonderful feeling of metal closed in around him as he slumped into the mud.

The last thing he saw was the gate falling, his parents on the other side, trying to get to him, held back by guards.

It was an image he took down into blackness.
It was the last time he would ever see them.

Southern California—1986

The rough, water-colored mural of the blue sky,
white clouds, and distant horizons hung on hooks
from the ceiling of the gym, just behind the basketball backboard, vibrating to the loud music. The
bottom third of the large painting was a crude drawing of a city skyline, with silhouettes of buildings in
gray paint and black outline. The most recognizable
shape was of the Statue of Liberty. Someone had even
cut a hole where her torch would be and had put a
light bulb there.

In front of the painting, high school kids danced, ate
at tables, and shouted over the music at the annual
"Rhapsody in Blue" prom. The tablecloths were blue,
the napkins were blue, and most of the girls had on far
too much blue eye shadow. Over half the boys' tuxes
were powder blue, though under the blue lights that
filled the air and lit the background of the gym, the
tuxes looked dark and faded.

Scott Summers stood facing Selena Ki, his date, just
to the right of the dance floor. He was thin and lanky,
with thick brown hair. His smile and friendly personality made him popular among most of the kids. So far,
in all the years of high school, he'd made every official
dance. At seventeen, this was his second "Rhapsody in
Blue" prom.

Selena was considered one of the best-looking girls in
the school. One of the school's cheerleaders, she pretty

much could have gone out with anyone she wanted. Scott felt lucky she had said yes when he asked her the first time.

He and Selena had been going out for at least a month. Scott liked her, but he was having trouble with her jealousy. Two of his friends had warned him about that problem, but he hadn't listened. Now he wished he had. If he even looked at another girl she got angry. And right now she was really, really mad.

"I don't ever want to talk to you again!" Selena shouted at Scott over the music.

"But—" Scott tried to say. Too late. She had already turned and stormed away through the crowd, her full, blue-and-white dress skirt brushing dancers out of the way.

He went after her, ignoring a few friends who stood to the side, shaking their heads.

Scott couldn't believe this was happening, not during the prom. So what if he'd talked to Bonnie yesterday after class? He was here with Selena, wasn't he? He didn't even like Bonnie. She'd just come up to him, said "Hi." But then, worst of all, she had given him a hug, right in front of Selena.

Was it his fault that Bonnie was a hugging kind of person?

It seemed Selena thought it was. She wasn't even allowing him the opportunity to explain. Or talk to her at all. And the night was still young. They still had dancing to do, plus two other parties.

This was so stupid. And it was beginning to make him mad.

She stormed out into the hall and stopped, with

Scott right behind her. At least out here the music level was almost bearable. Maybe out here she would let him explain that nothing was going to come between them.

He had almost reached her when she spun off and slipped into the girls' room.

He stared after her and set his jaw grimly. That wasn't going to stop him. Not this time.

He started for the door.

"Scott?" a voice said, bringing him up just before he was about to enter.

He glanced around and found Mr. Daniels, his math teacher from third period.

Daniels pointed to the men's room, just a few steps away. "Don't you think you'd be more comfortable in there?"

"Yeah," Scott said. "But I have to talk to her."

Daniels nodded. "I understand that. But just not in there. Trust me, eventually they all come out."

Despite the logic of what Daniels was saying, Scott was so mad he didn't know what to do.

And he was frustrated. Why was she doing this to him? What had he done to deserve having his night ruined, all because of her irrational fit of jealousy?

Suddenly, a jabbing pain shot through the back of his head and into his eyes.

"Ahhhh," he said, bending over, covering his eyes as they started to water.

"You all right, Summers?" Daniels asked.

Scott managed to nod, then quickly headed for the men's room. The pain was intense. So intense that his eyes felt as if they were trying to explode out of his head.

Inside the men's room about half a dozen others were smoking and laughing. The room was filled with the gray smoke. Scott bumped against a wall near the sink. The agony seemed to echo around inside his head.

Stan Hensey moved over and stood beside him as Scott pressed his eyes, trying to will the pain away. Stan and Scott had been friends for years, even though Stan hung out most of the time with the druggies.

"Selena, huh?" Stan asked. "You need to lighten up, dude. She's just a girl."

Scott shook his head. "Not her. My head. My eyes!"

"What's wrong with your eyes?" Stan asked, putting a hand on Scott's shoulder. "I got some contact lotion. Might help."

"Thanks." Scott stood and carefully opened his eyes.

"Holy—" Stan said, stumbling back. The look on his face was one of complete terror.

Scott wiped the tears away as the pain got worse and worse. "What's wrong?" He could still see Stan, but everything seemed strange, as if he were peering through a red haze.

"Your eyes, man," Stan said, still backing away. "They're red. *Really* red. Pupils and all."

Two other guys in the room glanced over at Scott, then jerked back.

Suddenly Scott could feel the pain come together at a point above the bridge of his nose. And then it vanished, as if it hadn't been there at all. Instead there was energy, flowing in his head. Energy he could feel like water running through his fingers.

Energy that wanted out.

For an instant it felt as if the entire inside of his head

was flowing out his eyes. The energy burst out through them, smashing into the wall in front of him in a bright red beam of light.

The wall exploded.

And then a massive hole appeared. Scott could see inside the girls' rest room. Selena and three other girls screamed and jumped away from the mirror.

The wall on the other side of the girls' rest room exploded outward.

At that moment Scott realized he was the one who was doing the damage. His eyes were.

He closed them, jamming his hands over them, and dropped to the ground.

Once again the energy seemed to flow around and around inside his head, calm now, but waiting to be released again when he opened his eyes.

Well, he wasn't going to open them.

Around him the screams and shouts and yelling started. Shortly after that there were sirens. He never did get the chance to tell Selena he was sorry.

Kenya—1988

The deep blue of the sky made the sun look almost white. The heat came off the ground in waves, so even the scant shade under the thin trees seemed useless as shelter.

The tribal village filled an open area along the edge of the sparse forest; the dirt around the tents was baked dry and hard. A dozen children of different ages played a game of tag, touching each other with sticks, then running to avoid the one who was "it."

Ororo, a young girl of twelve with a white streak running through her dark hair, played with them. Ororo was proud of herself because so far she had been able to keep from getting tagged. Sweat was streaming off her head and arms, but she didn't care. She was having fun.

And Ororo loved the warm air, the slight breeze that dried her sweat, the bright sun. She just loved being outside and had for as long as she could remember. To her the sun, the rain, the winds had always been things of joy and pleasure. This game with the other children just provided another chance to play in the sun.

The game continued until suddenly she was in the wrong place at the wrong time. The tap of the stick on her arm was like an insect sting, and the laughter of the others told her she was it.

Ororo could feel fear grabbing at her stomach. The last time she had been tapped when they played this game, she hadn't been able to tag anyone else and had ended up being laughed at for days. She was used to being laughed at. She was different from the others, and they all knew it somehow. Though except for the white streak in her hair, she didn't know how she was different. But she too knew it.

Usually she didn't mind not playing with the others, staying apart and alone. But this time, since she was playing, she was going to make sure the laughing didn't happen again. She would tag someone else.

Two younger boys and a girl her age were standing a short distance away, taunting her to get them. She knew that all three of them were faster, far faster than she was. It would be a waste of time to chase them.

So she turned and headed the other way, running around one tent as fast as she could go, hoping to surprise someone.

The idea didn't work. The other kids there saw her coming and ran, faster than her.

All the kids in the village were faster than her, and they all knew it.

But she could still tag one of them if she got lucky.

For the longest time she kept trying, chasing, not giving up. The heat was making her pant. She knew she should stop and drink, but if she did the game would end and she would be laughed at again.

They were already starting to laugh, and to call her names. And the more they laughed, the harder she tried.

Then things got worse. As she lunged to try to catch one younger boy, she tripped.

Ororo put her hands under her to catch herself. The sound of her stick snapping was like a slap from a tribal elder against her cheek.

Ororo pushed herself back to her feet, the brown dirt sticking to her sweating arms and legs. Her stick was broken in half. Now there was no way she could win. No way at all.

One of the kids saw what had happened, and in a moment, before she could even look up from her broken stick, they had all surrounded her, laughing, poking at her with their sticks.

"Stop!" she shouted, but that just made them laugh even harder, taunting her that she was too slow to make them stop, that she had broken her stick. And with her stick broken, how could she tag them?

Ororo was getting angrier and angrier as the others kept poking at her. Then one of them hit her.

The hit stung like a bee.

It sounded like someone had snapped their fingers. She could feel the pain of it coming off her shoulder.

She tried to move away, but they wouldn't let her, keeping her surrounded, hitting her more and more.

Snap! Snap!

Each hit hurt really bad. "Stop!" she shouted. "Stop it now!"

They laughed and hit her again and again.

And each hit hurt her more and more, until it became one big stinging pain on her back and shoulders and arms.

They were all hitting her with their sticks, telling her to run. They wanted to see her run.

But Ororo knew she couldn't outrun them, so she just stood there, turning to avoid the hits as best she could, as she would avoid the stings of swarming insects.

They laughed and yelled at her to run. It had become a new game of sorts, and she had become the object of the game.

Snap! Snap! Snap! The sticks whipped at her skin, drawing blood in places, raising welts in others.

Her voice was getting louder and louder. "Stop it! Stop it!"

But that, too, just made them hit her harder and harder.

Why were they doing this to her?

All Ororo wanted them to do was stop.

Why couldn't they just leave her alone? She could feel her face getting hot from the anger.

All she wanted to do was hit them all back, show them how it felt.

How it hurt.

But they kept on, and it seemed to go on forever.

As Ororo got angrier and angrier, she could feel the air around her clutching at her, pulling her.

Snap! Snap-snap-snap! The hits were coming even faster now, the laughter less and less.

She spun and moved, trying to get out of the way of each hit, usually failing.

She cried, and the nightmare continued.

Between sobs, she yelled at them to stop.

They kept going.

She wished for something to stop them.

Then everything changed. The hitting slowed, then stopped, as the other children looked up in awe at what was happening around them. The sky was falling, in big white flakes.

White, cold flakes in the heat of the afternoon, out of the blue, cloudless sky.

They fell slowly at first. Then faster, harder.

But none of the snow was falling on her. She was so angry, so racked with sobs, that she didn't notice, didn't care what was happening. Her shoulders and arms still stung where the other kids had hit her, and she wanted the sky to keep falling on them all, to hurt them all.

Gradually the white flakes falling from the clear, blue, cloudless heavens turned heavier, then became small chunks of ice.

The kids picked up the ice, looked at it. They laughed, staring upward as it pounded down.

It was still fun for them.

She dropped to the dry ground, sobbing as around her the falling ice got larger, still not touching her. Just them.

She stared at the other kids, the force of her anger more overwhelming than any she had ever felt. It had built up in her for years, like water behind a dam. And now the dam had burst, and she was letting all the anger flow. She had wanted, more than anything, for the sky to fall on them. It was doing just that, but she wanted more.

She wanted them to hurt as she hurt.

The ice chunks coming from the cloudless heavens got larger and larger. Soon the other children began shouting in pain. They scattered, trying to run for the tents.

But now the chunks of ice were so large that they began knocking the kids down, smashing into the tents, breaking off limbs from the trees.

She cried even harder as the kids shouted and screamed for it to stop.

Now they knew how she felt.

Maybe next time they wouldn't torment her again.

Ororo looked around, and it dawned upon her that the flakes of sky and ice hadn't hit her.

She put her head down in the dirt, feeling the ground and the comfort of the solidness. Every part of her back and arms hurt, yet the anger was ebbing. In its place was a deep feeling of knowing the winds and rains, of understanding the clouds and the sky. She could feel the water in the earth and the energy of the sun. All felt comforting. Deep inside she understood them, knew them all, as if they were her friends.

And as if she were theirs.

It wasn't until much later that she learned that, at that moment, her hair had turned as white as the falling sky.

Mississippi—The Not-Too-Distant Future

Marie traced the line on the map while pointing with her other hand to the picture of the Statue of Liberty on her bedroom wall. She had spent hours staring at that statue, and at the map, dreaming of traveling there, seeing the sights. Now she was sharing her dream with David.

David was from her school, and at sixteen, the same age. They had just started to date.

"I want to spend time in New York City," Marie said, smiling at David. He was sitting on the edge of her bed. Her parents were downstairs watching television and the door was open, but it still felt odd to have him in her room. Exciting, too. Only a few of her girlfriends had ever seen the inside of her bedroom.

"You going to live there?" David asked.

"No," she said, tracing the map farther north. "Niagara Falls, then into Canada. Toronto, west to Calgary, then on to Anchorage."

"Wow," David said, clearly impressed. He stood and moved over beside her, staring at the map. "Won't it be kinda cold?"

"Of course it will," she said, laughing. "Otherwise it wouldn't be an adventure."

She could feel his closeness, his shoulder rubbing against her shoulder.

"When are you gonna do this?"

Marie shrugged. "I don't know. After school, but before college."

He reached over and rested his hand on her shoulder. She could feel it, almost like a hot iron touching her, yet it didn't burn. It excited her, made her stomach twist like it had never twisted before. She had never been this close to a boy before. Not like this.

Not in her bedroom with her parents downstairs.

"So," she said, turning to face him a little, "what do you want to do now?"

He looked right into her eyes. Then he smiled, sending shivers down her back.

"I don't know," he said. "What do you want to do?"

He moved closer to her, and she could smell him. She was having trouble breathing, yet there was no way in the world she wanted him to move away.

"I don't know," she managed.

He turned her slightly so they were facing each other, then slowly he moved forward until he was kissing her.

It was as if a surge of electricity shot through every nerve cell in her body.

A thousand thoughts flashed through her mind.

He tastes good.

My parents are downstairs.

What will my friends think?

His lips feel wonderful.

I can't breathe.

I want to kiss him harder.

Then suddenly it all changed.

As she put her arms around him, kissing him back, suddenly his mind opened up to her.

She knew what he was thinking, knew what he liked,

what he hated, what he liked to do with the guys, what he wanted them to do.

David's eyes snapped open.

His hands locked around her in a terrifying grip.

She tried to pull away, but it felt as if he were pouring his every thought, his every wish, his every dream into her head.

Energy crackled around them, until finally she managed to pull away.

He dropped to the floor, his eyes open wide.

The next thing she knew she was screaming. The images of David's life were still tumbling in her head, filling her mind, mixing with her own until she almost couldn't tell which were hers and which were his.

He lay on the floor, twitching. It didn't look like he was breathing.

Had she killed him?

She hadn't done anything!

Her parents slammed into the room behind her as she realized she was still screaming, backed against the wall, staring at his body. She tried to push his memories away without success.

Her father immediately dropped to the floor and checked David, then started CPR.

Her mother came to her, but Marie didn't want her mother to touch her.

"I didn't mean to," she said softly.

Inside her head, his memories fought with hers. His images of her fought with how she saw herself. What he had wanted to do shocked her.

"Honey, what happened?" her mother asked desperately.

"Call a damned ambulance!" her father shouted.

Her mother jumped, then ran for the door as her father gave David mouth-to-mouth, then pumped his chest.

Marie pushed herself against the wall. She so wanted David to be all right. So wanted his memories and thoughts to leave her mind.

"I didn't do anything," she said, softly. But inside, she knew that she had.

She just didn't know what.

Chapter
One

Washington, DC—One Year Later

The cold of the winter day was long forgotten inside the Senate Hearing Room, as the packed bodies in the gallery and the heat from the television lights forced the temperature in the room up far above normal. Several of the senators, despite the intense media scrutiny of these hearings, had taken off their jackets. Many viewers in the balcony were fanning themselves with notebooks or loose paper.

Professor Charles Xavier sat in his wheelchair near the center of the room, watching patiently. He could tell that the crowd was a very hostile one. He didn't need to read their minds to sense that. Their hostility clearly emerged with every action of the hearings' chairman, the flamboyant senator Robert Kelly.

Kelly was a white-faced, white-haired man who was clearly using the hearings on mutant registration to propel his own career closer to the White House. And it seemed as though he had other demons that were driving him, though it wasn't quite clear to Professor Xavier what those demons were. At least not yet.

In front of the hot room, at the witness table, sat Dr.

Jean Grey. Even alone at the long wooden table, she had a commanding presence. A strong, good-looking woman in her early thirties, she had been called upon to explain to the Senate Hearing the basic science behind the emergence of mutants.

Professor Xavier had helped her extensively with the drafting of her presentation. They had gone over it time and again so that it would be clear not only to the senators, but to the audience on the other side of the television cameras.

And considering the hot-button interest the public had taken in the mutant registration law, there was no doubt her presentation would make the news. To many, mutants had proved ripe for persecution based on the long-standing tradition of fearing anything unknown. So the best defense, Jean and the professor had determined, was to help the regular people from middle America understand mutants and what they really were. The bigots like Senator Kelly would fold like wet tissue if public opinion shifted against them.

But for the moment, the public was squarely against mutants. And the public was scared to death. Senator Kelly was a master of playing that to the hilt.

"Lights, please?" Jean said.

A few people murmured something about that helping the heat, at least.

As the lights dimmed around him, the professor didn't need to shift in his wheelchair to watch the show. Instead he focused his gaze straight ahead and opened his mind, to let the feelings of those around him flow in, but only a little. Not enough to read their thoughts—just enough to gauge how reaction to the presentation was going.

He could feel boredom and hostility. Jean had a very deep hole to climb out of, it seemed. They all did, if they were ever going to be accepted by society and defeat this registration law.

"DNA," Jean said, spacing each letter as she started her presentation. "It is the basic building block of evolution. Changes in our DNA are the reason we have evolved from single-celled organisms to *Homo sapiens*."

Figures on the screen showed the various stages of evolution, along with a graph displaying a diagonal line that indicated the ascent of the human animal: the evolution of man.

One image took over the screen, focusing attention on the lowest order of humanoid: *Homo habilis*, a primitive apelike humanoid covered in thick hair.

Around him, Professor Xavier could feel the crowd's interest increase, ever so slightly. And some revulsion emerged, as men and women confronted images of what they were descended from.

"Within our DNA," Jean said, explaining what was happening on the screen, "are the genes that decide our physical characteristics. When these active genes mutate, we see changes in the body."

The image on the screen began to mutate, and the apelike humanoid slowly started looking more and more human.

The professor could tell many of the people around him were becoming fascinated. Perfect. It was just what he and Jean had hoped would be their reaction at this point.

"These evolutionary changes are subtle, and normally take thousands of years."

The image of the now-human man on the screen froze, and his body went transparent. Twenty percent of it was marked in blue, representing moving, active genes. The remainder of the image of the man was marked in red, showing static, dormant genes.

Now the people around the professor were really caught up. The room fell silent, except for a few whispers coming from a couple of the senators who clearly were not paying any attention and didn't want to.

One of them was the chairman, Senator Kelly.

"Within each of us," Jean said, "lie not only the millions of genes which dictate our physical makeup, but millions upon millions more whose purpose has been completely unknown to us."

She paused for a breath, then went on. "These unused genes have traditionally been referred to as 'junk DNA.' In fact, over eighty percent of our genetic structure is made up of this so-called junk DNA."

The words PRESENT DAY appeared on the screen, as a number of the red, dormant genes began to move, slowly at first, then faster and faster.

"In recent years," Jean said, "and for reasons which are still a mystery, we have seen this latent DNA in our bodies mutating. These mutations manifest at puberty, and are often triggered by periods of heightened emotional stress."

With a glow of pride, the professor knew that—at this moment—with the exception of a few of the closed-minded senators, Jean had her audience. Despite the heat, they were paying rapt attention.

"The new DNA strands caused by the mutations are producing some admittedly startling results. In other words, this previously unused DNA is not 'junk' DNA at all, but rather a vast storehouse which contains the almost limitless potential for human advancement."

Suddenly the graphic on the screen showed the man performing amazing feats. First he grew in size; then he moved an object with his mind; then he changed the color of his skin.

"Ladies and gentlemen, we are now seeing the beginnings of another stage of human evolution. Not a new race of creatures to be feared, but rather the opportunity to find advancement within us all."

The lights slowly brightened.

Scanning the room once again, the professor could tell that Jean and the presentation had accomplished what they had hoped. With understanding, the perception of mutants seemed to have begun to shift ever so subtly. The professor began to pick up feelings of uncertainty, of people rethinking their positions. And the level of hostility was clearly lower. But now came the hard part. Jean had to hold this hard-won ground against Senator Kelly.

Kelly turned from the man he'd been talking to and smiled at Jean, like a father might smile at a small child who had just done something cute. "Thank you for the wonderful cartoon, Ms. Grey," he said in a vaguely patronizing tone. "It was quite—how should I say it?—educational."

Some of the crowd snickered.

"However," Kelly went on, "it failed to address the larger issue which, I might add, is the focus of this hearing. Three words: Are mutants dangerous?"

There was a low rumbling among the crowd, and the professor could feel new and increased uncertainty flowing among the people.

"Well, Senator Kelly," Jean responded, "don't you think that's an unfair question? The wrong person behind the wheel of a car can be dangerous."

"Well," Kelly countered, "we do license people to drive."

The professor listened carefully to the murmurs of the crowd as Senator Kelly's aide, Henry Guyrich, moved behind the panel and handed Kelly a black folder filled with documents.

"But we don't license people to live, Senator," Jean said.

Kelly said nothing.

"It is fact, Senator," Jean said, pressing her point, "that mutants who have revealed themselves publicly have been met with fear, hostility, and even violence."

The professor could feel that things were again turning against Jean. This time, though, as he scanned the crowd with his mind, he felt a new presence, a powerful and familiar one. He turned around in his wheelchair and studied the back of the room, which rose above him.

There, by the door, in the shadows where he couldn't be seen, stood a dark figure wearing a very expensive suit.

It was his old friend Eric. What was he doing here?

The professor nodded, and Eric did the same. The professor turned back to face the front, his attention again on the crowd.

"It is because of that ever-present hostility," Jean said, "that I am urging the Senate to vote against mutant registration. To force mutants to expose themselves will only further subject them to unnecessary prejudice."

Senator Kelly smiled and wiped a drop of sweat from the side of his head. The professor could tell he was going to attack Jean, and attack her hard—as they had expected.

"Expose themselves?" Kelly asked, his voice calm and strong over the silent crowd as he played to the television cameras. "What is it that the mutant community has to hide?"

"I didn't say they had anything to hide," Jean said. "What I did say—"

"Let me show you what's being hidden," Senator Kelly said, talking over Jean without hesitation. He raised a blown-up photo of a car on a freeway. The car appeared to have been melted. "This was taken by a state police officer in Secaucus, New Jersey. A man in a minor altercation literally melted the car in front of him."

Professor Xavier set his jaw. The crowd was again turning fearful, and hostile. More and more fans were back at work trying to cool the heat.

"May I see that photo, Senator?" Jean asked calmly.

He ignored her question and spoke to the cameras and crowd. "This is not an isolated incident, Ms. Grey."

Kelly picked up the folder filled with documents and held it up for the crowd to see. "I have a list of names here. Identified mutants, living right here in the United States."

"Senator Kelly!" Jean said, her voice becoming more forceful.

But he just ignored her. "A girl in Illinois who can walk through walls. What is to stop her from walking into a bank vault? Or even the White House?"

Senator Kelly, an intense look of concern pasted on his face, pointed out at the crowd and the cameras. "Or your house?"

Professor Xavier knew, right at that moment, that they had lost. The crowd's anger and hostility were back in full force. Heated discussions and scattered debates erupted throughout the chamber. Senator Kelly was getting them to ignore the facts and focus on their own fears of the unknown.

Jean tried to shout over the noise, to engage the senator. "You are not being—"

"And there are even rumors, Ms. Grey," Kelly said, turning to stare directly at her, "of mutants so powerful that they can enter our minds and control our thoughts, taking away our God-given free will."

A number of people actually gasped at that statement.

"Ms. Grey, Americans deserve the right to decide whether they want their children to be in school with mutants. To be taught by mutants." Kelly leaned forward. "You're a schoolteacher. I would think that the rights of parents and students alike should be of paramount importance to you."

"They are," Jean said firmly. "But this is not the way to help them. I would like to see that folder."

"Why?" Kelly asked, pounding the folder, then waving it in front of the crowd. "All I'm saying is that parents have the right to know the dangers to their children. That's the purpose of registration."

"It is not the purpose," Jean shouted, clearly angry now. "Your purpose is to discriminate and torture a group of citizens, just because you are afraid of them.

Now I would like to see your so-called list and evidence."

She held her hand out.

Suddenly the folder flew from Kelly's grasp toward Jean's open hand.

Realization swept across her face, and Jean instantly closed her hand and let her arm fall to her side. But the professor knew the damage had been done. The folder dropped to the floor, photos and papers spilling out.

Around him, the professor could tell that everyone was uncertain what had happened. And they were very afraid at the same time. It was clear to all of them that something unseen had come into play in this hearing, though none of them knew what it might be.

The professor sighed and closed down his mind, shutting out the sensations of the people around him. They had lost this battle, that much was clear.

"Ladies and gentlemen," Senator Kelly said, now more than ever playing for the cameras. "The truth is that mutants are very real and that they are among us. We must know who they are, and above all, we must know what they can do."

The crowd broke into cheering around the professor as he turned and moved his wheelchair up the ramp toward the exit. It had been a long shot, and he knew it.

From the almost-empty hallway outside the Hearing Room, the professor could hear the debate continuing as a few friendly senators tried to jump in to help Jean. But they were quickly overwhelmed. It was clear that this bill would leave this hearing and make its way to the main floor of the Senate. That would be the next point at which it might be stopped. But he was going to have to do better, if that was to happen.

In front of the professor, a man walked toward the main entrance. Eric Lehnsherr.

"What are you doing here?" the professor asked, just loud enough for Eric to hear.

Lehnsherr stopped and half turned, smiling.

"Why do you ask questions when you already know the answer?" Lehnsherr asked.

The professor moved up closer, until they faced each other there in the high-ceilinged, tiled hallway. "Don't give up on them, Eric."

"What would you have me do, Charles?" he asked. "I've heard all these arguments before. Used very well, if I remember."

"That was a long time ago," the professor said. "Mankind has evolved since then."

"Yes," Eric said. "Into us."

The professor paused a moment, musing, then decided to seek out what he wanted to know. Slowly and carefully, he reached out.

Eric put a palm against the side of his head, then smiled. "Are you sneaking around in here, Charles?"

Eric clenched his fist, and the professor's chair pressed inward, as if it had suddenly been gripped by a giant hand. Then the chair seemed to lift ever so slightly off the ground, as if in a subtle warning.

"Whatever are you looking for?" Eric asked, still smiling, but adding an edge to his words.

"Hope, Eric," the professor said calmly. "I'm looking for hope."

The chair settled back to the tile floor, as if the hand had released it.

"I will bring you hope," Eric said. "And I only ask one thing in return: Don't get in my way."

Eric Lehnsherr turned and walked away. Without looking back, he said, "We are the future, Charles. Not them. They no longer matter."

Behind him the professor could hear the debate continuing as his former ally pushed open the door and left. He hadn't responded to that last comment, because there was nothing left to be said. He didn't agree, and Eric knew it.

Regular people did matter. Now more than ever.

Chapter Two

Alberta, British Columbia, Canada

The snow was falling steadily, a light powder—the only kind that could fall in such extreme temperatures. Even though it was still daylight, the spotlight over the front door of the Lion's Den Bar and Grill was on. It cut through the snow but did little to illuminate the few cars in the lot, the four eighteen-wheelers that had been parked along the road, or the beat-up camper that was sitting axle-deep in a small drift. Attached to the back of the camper was an old trailer full of cord wood and a rusted motorcycle. A small hand-lettered sign on the trailer read, "Firewood for Sale."

The inside of the Lion's Den was as anyone might expect from the outside: low lighting, smoke filled, far too many calendars decorating the walls beside old signs, and animal heads covered in dust and grease. This place was divided between a cafe on one side and a bar on the other, with dirty bathrooms through doors in the back.

Logan had been in a hundred places just like this one. They all had decent food that the locals liked, served in large portions. The drinks were strong, and the regulars didn't much like strangers. In every one of the places, Logan had been a stranger, stopping to eat and have a few drinks, then moving on. He couldn't imagine ever settling down long enough to become a regular anywhere.

He had just finished eating on the cafe side of the joint, sitting in a booth, downing three cups of coffee with his steak. Now he was at the bar, two stools down from an old, very unused jukebox. A few drinks and he would be headed down the road again. There was still plenty of time left in the day to make some miles. He had nowhere in particular he was going; he just liked to keep moving. It felt better that way.

Unlike the cafe side, with its smell of French fries and chicken-fried steak, the bar stank of stale beer and too many cigarettes. The floor was a dirty tile, and the tables were all scarred with carved-in initials and epithets. At the moment there were four patrons sitting at two tables, staring at him. They were clearly regulars.

Drunk regulars.

He had ignored them when he came in, and he did the same now, sitting with his back to the main room and the main door. He knew he looked weird to most people: too much hair, an animal-like face. He got a lot of stares and had long since given up caring.

The bartender, a man with a round, scarred face, moved in behind the bar. Logan was just about to motion him over when some loud, foot-stomping truck drivers came in. There was a grimy mirror set in the wall behind the bottles of booze at the bar, and Logan could see that there were four truckers, big gutted and no doubt smelling of too many miles on the road. Logan was glad he wasn't close enough to catch that odor.

The four were escorting a girl. Clearly she had been riding with them. They were all laughing, paying no attention, but Logan watched as her eyes quickly sized up the place. No smile ever crossed her face. He guessed that she was a runaway, and she was dressed in rags, head to toe, with almost every inch of her skin covered. Only her face and hands showed any exposed skin. He wondered what she was hiding—then reminded himself to mind his own business.

For Logan, minding his own business was what kept him going.

He tapped his after-dinner cigar in the ashtray, then motioned for the bartender.

"Yeah?" the scarred man asked. He moved toward Logan, while nodding to the truck drivers over Logan's shoulder. "What can I get you?"

"Something on tap," Logan said.

"What kind?"

"Surprise me," Logan said wryly.

The bartender turned away without so much as a blink. He was a big guy who nonetheless moved smoothly, which gave the impression he was moving slowly instead. Logan had no doubt the bartender had taken care of himself in more than one fight in this place.

The truck drivers crowded into a booth, with the young girl sitting on a chair facing them. Logan could hear them laughing again, but he paid no attention at all to what they were saying.

In front of him, a TV was bolted to the wall in the corner above the back bar. The news was on.

"Preparations are nearly completed for the upcoming United Nations World Summit," the announcer said. "With nearly every invitation confirmed, the event promises to be the largest single gathering of world leaders in history."

Logan watched as the image on the screen changed from the announcer's bland face to an aerial shot of Ellis Island, with the Statue of Liberty and Liberty Island close by in the background.

"The leaders of over two hundred nations will discuss issues ranging from the world's economic climate and weapons treaties, to the mutant phenomenon and its impact on our world stage."

Logan snorted, then shook his head. This mutant thing really had people spooked if it was coming down to discussing it at a world conference. And scared people had a habit of becoming dangerous.

The bartender put Logan's beer down in front of him, then turned to move away.

"There anything else on?"

The bartender shrugged and headed for the television. "Satellite's busted. Only got two channels."

He changed it from the news to a fuzzy image of a rerun of some stupid sitcom.

"That all right?"

"Perfect," Logan said, taking a swig of his beer. It was cold and tasted fresh. At least places like this usually had good local brews. Good food, good beer— what more could a guy ask for?

"Hey, Joe," one of the drunk-sounding regulars shouted.

The bartender looked up and frowned.

"You ever seen a mutant, Joe?" the regular asked, pointing at the television and slurring his words.

Joe casually tossed the towel over his shoulder as he moved to take the truck drivers' order. "There's no mutant dumb enough to walk in here."

"Got that right," the drunk agreed.

Logan watched in the mirror, sipping his beer and smoking his cigar, as the bartender talked with the drivers. He asked the young girl if she wanted something. She shook her head, then stood and came toward Logan and the bar.

He masked his curiosity as she moved in close to him. He could smell her unwashed odor. Clearly she had been on the road for some time and hadn't been out of the clothes long enough to clean them.

He could also sense the fear in her. Deep fear.

"Listen, can you help me?" she asked quietly. "Please? I was hitchhiking and these guys won't let me go. I think they're gonna try to—"

"Hey!" one of the truck drivers said loudly.

Logan watched him in the mirror. He was a big guy, and he stood and moved toward the bar. This guy moved like a lumbering elephant, though. Logan sized him up and decided that even the girl could take him.

"I thought you were just going to the bathroom," the trucker said to the girl. The tone of his voice clearly indicated that he had decided the girl was his property.

The girl looked at Logan, panic showing clearly in her eyes, the smell of fear spreading from her like a wave of sickness, choking the air.

Logan just sipped his beer, trying to ignore her.

Minding his own business was how he managed to get along, and minding his own business right now was exactly what he was planning to do. He had his own troubles, and she had hers.

Life was just tough that way.

"Come on, honey," the truck driver said. He reached out and grabbed her arm.

She pulled back, hard. Freaked. "Don't touch me! I told you, don't touch me!"

He grabbed at her again, catching her hand. "I said come on. Do as I say!"

The instant he touched her hand, there was a flash. Not much of one, but enough to surprise Logan.

Then the trucker's eyes went wide, as if he was in shock. An instant later, he collapsed with a thud into a heap on the floor.

Logan glanced down at where the trucker lay twitching. His mouth and eyes were open, but his expression was blank. Then Logan turned his attention back to the girl, who was shaking in fear and anger. "Nice job," he murmured.

"I told him not to touch me," she said softly.

The other three truckers had realized what had happened, and they moved fast for an overweight bunch of middle-aged rednecks.

"Hank?" one of them said tentatively, kneeling beside the twitching body on the floor.

The girl instinctively stepped closer to Logan, standing between the bar stools. Her stink was putting him right off his beer.

"Get his head up," one of the other truckers ordered anxiously.

Logan laughed inwardly. That was always good

advice if a person might have a broken neck. It would kill them instantly.

"I'll call an ambulance," Joe the bartender said in an almost bored fashion, then he turned to the phone on the back bar. Logan was starting to like good old Joe more and more.

While two of the big guys tried to get their friend breathing regularly again, the third stood and moved up to Logan. "You wanna tell me what happened?"

Logan shrugged, tapping his cigar in the ashtray and glancing down at the still-twitching trucker without turning fully around. "I don't know."

"What do you mean you don't know?" the guy demanded.

Logan watched the guy's hands clench up into fists. Clearly the man wanted a fight. This just might turn out to be a good day after all.

"Maybe he's sleepy," Logan said sarcastically. "How would I know?"

The trucker grabbed the back of Logan's shirt and spun him around on the stool. "What? Are you trying to be funny? Come on, just give me an excuse to stomp your tail."

Logan put his cigar down in the ashtray. It still had half way to burn, and he didn't want to waste it. Then with a quick spin, he drove his elbow directly into the trucker's face. The feeling of smashing flesh and the sound of the guy's nose breaking were beautiful. Pure poetry.

The trucker dropped to the tiled floor faster than his friend had. Logan shook his head. These guys were big, which meant they had more weight pulling them down. And clearly they had no threshold for pain.

"That excuse enough for you?" Logan asked the driver as he lay there, clutching at his nose.

The other two were on Logan quick, considering their size. He let them pin his arms, let them think they had him, as they held him one on each side. If they really wanted a fight, he might as well enjoy himself a little. Might not get this chance again for a while.

The guy with the busted nose slowly climbed to his feet and faced Logan, who was now pinioned between the trucker's two friends. Blood streamed down the guy's chin and dripped on his fat gut, turning his already stained shirt dark.

Logan just smiled.

That infuriated the guy even more, and he reared back. He put his anger behind his fist and hit Logan square in the face.

Logan moved his head slightly, timing the turn with the punch. The blow hit him solidly across the chin. He'd felt worse before. Not only was this guy fat, he was weak on top of it.

The guy looked surprised, and held his hand as if he had hurt it. More than likely the idiot had.

The two who thought they were holding Logan clutched tighter.

Logan shook his head from side to side. "That was pathetic," he said.

The broken-nosed trucker took another full swing, this time hitting Logan in the gut.

Logan doubled over, pretending the guy had actually hurt him. As he was bent over, he clenched his fists and pushed the knuckles of each hand against a leg of one of his captors.

Then he popped his claws.

Nine inches of metal shot from each knuckle.

Eight razor-sharp claws stabbed through cloth, skin, and muscle as if it weren't there.

The sound of metal echoed across the room.

Logan pulled his claws back in quickly. Both truckers suddenly shouted in pain and let go, each grabbing his leg.

The bloody-nosed trucker stared at his two friends as they collapsed to the floor and screamed in pain, blood flowing from their legs.

"What did you do?" he demanded, panic beginning to edge into his voice.

Logan stepped toward the man. He was no longer grinning. "You always ask the same stupid question?"

The guy backed away, slowly, grabbing glasses off of tables and throwing them on the ground between them. Then he picked up a metal bar tray, holding it between himself and Logan.

Logan's fist shot out. His claws extended again and skewered the tray. He yanked it out of the trucker's hand and tossed it away.

Then Logan grabbed the man's bloodied shirt, shoving the guy's head hard against the rough wooden wall. He was going to scare this guy, and scare him good.

While holding his opponent against the wall, he held up his fist, claws extended. Then he reared back and made a forward motion, as if to punch the guy, claws and all.

Behind him, the girl screamed as his claws sank into the wall on both sides of the guy's neck. His middle claw had withdrawn just enough so that it only pricked the surface of the guy's neck.

The trucker looked as if he might faint, or be sick. Either way, this just wasn't fun any longer. What Logan really wanted to do was fight. So he withdrew his claws.

"Run," he said into the trucker's face.

The man tripped over himself as he scrambled for the door, clearly not caring about his friends, who were still writhing in pain on the floor.

Logan took the moment to glance around. The girl also was gone, and the bartender looked terrified now. The other drunk customers were still sitting at their tables, petrified with shock.

Logan moved back up to the bar. "Sorry about the mess, but they started it," he said, nodding at the men on the floor. "Add the repairs to their check."

He picked up his half-finished cigar, put enough money on the bar to pay for his beer, and headed out into the snow. There was still time to make some miles.

Outside, he stopped and looked around. The girl was nowhere to be seen.

Too bad for her. He might have offered her a ride if she'd waited around long enough for him to get finished with his fun.

He shrugged and climbed into his camper, turning the key and gunning it to life. Then he drove hard and fast through the snow to get it out onto the road. He was a half mile down the highway when the odor reached him.

He took his cigar out of his mouth and sniffed again, just to be sure. Then he sighed and hit the brakes. No one was going to hitch a ride without his permission. He didn't care how young she was.

Or how much trouble she was in.

Chapter
Three

Alberta, British Columbia, Canada

Marie huddled under the tarp, shivering next to the cold metal of a motorcycle, as the camper slid to a stop on the slick road. For an instant she thought about making a run for it as fast as she could. But where would she go? Back to the truckers? The bar? It was snowing—she'd freeze to death before she got very far.

Maybe the guy was stopping for another reason. If she could just stay in here until they reached a town, then she would get out.

She still had the memories of the trucker swirling around in her head. She had a clear picture of what he had planned on doing to her. It disgusted her.

But the realization that he was planning on killing her, just as he had done to two other girls, scared her even more. She hadn't been this terrified since she had run away from home.

She knew what he had done to those girls, where their bodies were buried. Now she wished she had held the bastard longer, drained everything from him, so there would be no chance of him ever recovering. Just as his victims had not been given a chance.

Just as he hadn't been planning on giving her a chance.

There truly were some animals in this world, human animals, and she knew she was going to have to learn to deal with that if she stayed on the run.

She held her breath, trying not to move at all as the intense quiet of the Canadian wilderness closed in around the camper.

She sat there, scared and cold, waiting.

Ever since what happened to David in her bedroom, her life had been a waking nightmare. She had been scared more than not. And very lonely.

At first she had tried to pretend that nothing had really happened. She had pretended she hadn't been cursed with his every thought and memory. She had tried to convince herself that it had all been her scared mind, making things up.

And after a month or so, she had succeeded. David's memories and thoughts had faded from her consciousness, and David had recovered. Since everyone thought it was something wrong with David, no one said much, and the incident was kept quiet around school.

She had even come to think the same thing, fooling herself that it was something wrong with David.

Then, a few months later, she had ended up with Sean at the dance, caught in the moment, forgetting David and her first kiss altogether. For an instant the kiss with Sean had been wonderful, exciting. Like nothing else she had ever felt. Her heart had been pounding, her every nerve wound tight.

Then, just as with David, everything about Sean had

seemed to flow into her, as if she were draining him, like drawing water from a sink.

The next thing she knew, Sean was on the floor, his eyes wide. He was hardly breathing.

And she knew everything about him: his strengths, his habits, his loves.

She had stood over him saying over and over, "I didn't do anything. I didn't do anything."

The rest was a nightmare. People scrambled around her, trying to help Sean, get him to the hospital. She had tried to go back to school a few days later, but Sean's friends hadn't let her. They blamed her. Then, in defending herself, she had touched another person, and she had stolen more thoughts and memories.

And she'd left that person with eyes wide open, almost not breathing, lying on the floor.

She had hurt someone else.

Again.

At that moment she had realized, with terrifying clarity, that when she touched a person, she actually absorbed that person's thoughts, their memories, their life, even their abilities—everything about them. She hurt them, even though she didn't want to hurt them.

From that moment on, she couldn't stand the looks she was getting from people, even from her parents. The word "mutant" was starting to be whispered loudly when she passed. So the night after she had tried to go back to school, she had packed a few things, covered her body completely so no one could accidentally touch her bare skin, left her parents a good-bye note, and run away.

Now here she was, hiding in the stinking bathroom of a man who clearly had strange abilities, just like she did. She didn't know why she had gone to him for help in the bar. Something about him, even though he was the hairiest person she had ever seen, had seemed to draw her. He looked almost more animal than human, and when those claws had popped out of his fist, it had scared her.

So why was she here?

How he had easily dealt with the three truckers—that had scared her even more. While he finished the fight, she had run.

Outside in the snow she had seen the camper, supposing it must be his, figuring he would be leaving right behind her. She had thought it would be her best choice to get away from there. She could hide until he stopped in a town, then jump and run away.

But now, with the camper stopped on the side of the road, a good distance from anywhere, it didn't seem like such a good choice after all.

The door to the camper opened, and the trailer rocked as the hairy man climbed out. She could smell the biting odor of his cigar. Maybe he was just getting something, then would go back to driving.

She held her breath, not daring to make a sound.

"Get out!"

His voice seemed to come down on her like a sledgehammer. Her heart pounded. He knew she was here.

She eased back the tarp slowly and climbed out. The man with the black hair and claws stood there, facing her across the small space. The door to the camper was still open, and all around she could see dimly the white road and the shapes of trees through the falling snow.

"Where am I supposed to go?" she demanded with faint defiance.

"I don't know," the man said. "Get out."

She moved past him, the cold air biting at her face. "You don't know, or you don't care?"

"Pick one," he said. "Get out."

She stepped down into the snow and walked a few steps away, stopping behind the trailer.

The hairy man turned on his heels, got back into the camper, and slammed the door. A moment later the truck's tires were spinning as the camper pulled away.

She watched it for a moment, then glanced around. There was nothing out here. And the cold was already starting to bite at her. She was going to be lucky if she could even make it back to the bar.

At least they would blame him for the fight.

The camper's taillights were almost invisible in the snow when suddenly the brake lights flared. After a moment, a voice came though the snow.

"I can't wait forever."

She smiled. She had known there was something about this guy. For all his gruff exterior, he couldn't leave her to die out here.

She walked to where he was parked on the road and climbed into the passenger seat. "Thanks."

He didn't say anything as he shoved the camper back into gear and spun back into motion.

The silence in the cab was tense.

She sat, pushed against the door, grasping her seat belt, as he smoked his cigar and drove. The windshield wipers barely cleared the blowing snow, and she doubted he could see more than a car's length in front of them. Considering that the two-lane road was tree lined and had sudden curves, he was driving far too fast. But at this point, she certainly wasn't going to say anything.

"So, what's your name?" she asked tentatively.

The man chewed on his cigar for a moment, focusing all his attention on the road. Then he finally answered. "Logan. What's yours?"

She almost said Marie, then decided to stick with the name she had been trying to use since she left home.

"Rogue."

They sat in silence again for a long few moments. The snow seemed to be coming down even harder, and the *slap, slap, slap* of the windshield wipers counted the time as it passed like the blurry outlines of the trees.

Finally he said, "What kind of name is Rogue?"

She liked the name Rogue. She felt it suited her perfectly at the moment. "What kind of name is Logan?"

He nodded, chewing on the now-short stump of his cigar. "Good point."

Slap, slap, slap. The silence continued. Rogue wasn't sure if she should even be trying to talk to the man.

After a moment he tossed his old cigar butt into a full ashtray, then pulled a new smoke from under the seat and, while driving with his leg pressed against the steering wheel, lit the tip. The cab filled with clouds of fresh smoke, and he sighed. She wanted to open the window, get some fresh air blowing in here before she got sick to her stomach, but didn't know if she should even do that.

Finally she decided that trying to talk was better than sitting in frustrating silence.

"How long have you known?" she asked.

"Known what?" he asked back, glancing at her.

"That you were, you know, like me?" Rogue had heard that there were others with special powers like hers. Mutants. She just hadn't believed it.

"I'm not like you," the guy said, blowing a large cloud of smoke between his face and the windshield. She had no idea how he could see the road, but he seemed to be managing just fine.

"Right," Rogue said, laughing, "you're just a normal, everyday claw guy."

"Listen, kid," Logan said, "right now the only thing you've done to endear yourself to me is to get three big truckers to attack me. Now granted, that was kind of fun, so I'm cutting you some slack. Any more chatter and the slack runs out."

She smiled, staring through the snow at the faint outline of the mountain road. Then she said, "You know, you should wear your seat belt."

"What did I tell you?" he asked.

But she could tell he was almost smiling. Almost.

The next instant the world seemed to end.

Something big toppled in front of them from Logan's side, falling directly across the road.

He reacted, but he had no chance of success. The camper came to an almost-instant stop.

Rogue was smashed against her seat belt. Her head snapped forward, then backward, banging on the panel behind her.

Logan was tossed hard through the windshield, bouncing and tumbling down the road like a rag doll.

Out her side window the trailer full of wood and

the motorcycle shot past, tumbling end over end, the trailer's contents scattering like leaves in the wind.

To Rogue it seemed as if everything in the camper suddenly piled around her, shoving her forward. She could see Logan's body through the broken-out windshield. Snow swirled in and around her face as everything finally came to a stop.

They had hit a massive falling tree. The force of the impact had shoved it forward and to one side. From where she sat, it was clear that this truck wasn't going to be going anywhere again anytime soon. The hood and front end were wrapped around the log.

The silence now seemed almost heavy. She sat there, trying to catch her breath, trying to stop her heart from pounding out of her chest. It was the first time she had ever been in an automobile accident. It had happened so fast.

Then through the snow she saw movement.

Logan was alive. How was that possible?

In the road ahead, he climbed to his feet, brushing himself off. "Damn it!" he said.

She sat there, staring at him in shock. No one could live through being tossed through a truck windshield, then bouncing down the concrete like he had done. He had to be dead, or at least seriously injured. Yet here he was, walking toward her, swearing under his breath.

As he got closer, she could see that there were gashes in his cheek and forehead. Deep, bleeding cuts that were going to need treatment quickly.

Then, as she watched, the gashes stopped bleeding and began to heal up.

That wasn't possible.

Logan didn't even seem to notice, or think anything was

out of the ordinary. Then she realized that her ability—to take someone's thoughts, abilities, everything—also wasn't possible. Yet she did it.

"You all right?" Logan asked, stopping in front of the truck and staring at her through the windshield.

"I'm fine," she said, still not really wanting to move to check that claim out completely.

Logan nodded and studied the tree they had hit, walking along it toward the shattered trunk, shaking his head. From what Rogue could tell, the tree had come off the side of the cliff, probably brought down by the heavy snow.

She was still shaking so much that she didn't even want to try to move. Instead she just sat, trying to get herself to relax.

As Logan climbed up to check the base of the shattered tree, a hand punched out of a large snowdrift right beside him: a huge, clawed hand that grabbed him by the back of the jacket.

Rogue screamed as a snow-covered monster rose up, towering over Logan. It picked him up and swung him around, tossing him into the cliff side with enough force that Rogue could feel the ground shake even from where she was.

The creature stood there, staring at where it had thrown Logan. Rogue saw that it wasn't actually an animal, but a large man with long yellow hair, wearing animal hides. He had sharp teeth and cat's eyes, and he was the ugliest thing Rogue had ever seen.

As the creature stepped toward Logan, Rogue tried to move. The seat had been shoved forward and was jammed behind her by the camper. Her legs were trapped under the dashboard. The more she fought to get them free, the more it hurt.

She tried shoving the passenger door open, but it, too, was stuck, so she went back to feeling around her legs with her hands, trying to find anything she could move to get free.

Then behind her she heard a slight crackling sound.

She twisted around, expecting to see another creature, but what she saw through the cracked camper was something far worse.

Fire.

The camper was on fire.

She went back to fighting to free her legs.

Through the windshield she could see Logan emerge from the snow, clearly angry. With one backhand slap, the fur-covered man smashed Logan into a tree. How strong was this thing?

Logan came up rolling, his claws extended. "You want a fight? You're going to get a fight!"

Logan slashed at the man.

Missed.

Slashed again.

Missed again, as the man-creature moved quickly out of the way. The thing grabbed Logan's wrist and, using Logan's own forward momentum, picked him up and swung him 360 degrees, smashing him into the log.

The log shattered.

Rogue fought even harder now. She had to get away from the fire, from this mockery of a man.

Logan was stunned, but he still tried to stagger to his feet.

The huge man-creature picked Logan up like a

pillow, held him in the air, then tossed him twenty feet back through the remains of the truck's windshield.

Rogue managed to cover her face and turn slightly in the seat as Logan smashed into her, unconscious.

Behind her the fire spread, smoke pouring through the cab and up into the falling snow.

The man-creature stood, staring at her with its cat's eyes. They almost seemed to be glowing.

"Mister," Rogue said, shaking Logan. "Mister, wake up, okay?"

She shook him harder, making sure to touch only his clothes, while still trying to pull her legs free.

"Come on, come on," she said as the man-creature stepped toward the burning camper. "Please wake up."

Chapter Four

Alberta, British Columbia, Canada

Storm shifted awkwardly in the X-Men jet's seat, trying to get comfortable. Beside her in the pilot's seat, Cyclops dozed lightly, his visor strapped firmly to his face. The last two hours had dragged inexorably past, the white snow around them falling hard, covering everything. On the tracking monitor, their subject, Sabretooth, was still a half mile away, stopped.

Waiting. They had no idea for what, but he was clearly waiting. And so were they.

Sabretooth was a mutant whose abilities had manifested themselves as animal strength, speed, sight, and smell. From what Storm had learned in their premission briefing, Sabretooth had been helping Magneto. Why the professor had wanted them to track Sabretooth out here into the Canadian wilderness was anyone's guess. He certainly hadn't bothered to tell them, if he even knew.

But Storm didn't know a lot about the relationship between the professor and Magneto. All she had gleaned was that they seemed to be old friends, fighting in different ways for the same cause.

She and Cyclops had just been told to trail Sabretooth until something happened. They would know when it did, the professor had said.

She certainly hoped so.

Storm glanced around at the raging blizzard falling around the jet. She could see the nearby outline of a highway and the snow-covered trees and rocks. She could stop the snow around them if she wanted. But at the moment she didn't mind it at all. It was soothing, almost relaxing. She had a feeling about weather, could touch it, and almost any type of weather was good as far as she was concerned.

This snowstorm was certainly a far cry from the arid heat of her native Kenya. The first time she'd ever seen snow there was the day she had caused it.

The day the other kids of her village had tortured her.

The day she had come into her powers.

Thank heavens Professor Xavier had found her, or there would have been no telling what her people would have done to her after she had destroyed their village. She certainly had had no idea what to do with herself at that point.

No mutant did, when first coming into his or her powers. There was no way any of them could. It was something completely unexpected, and in this world that feared mutants, certainly none of them had been trained to cope.

Until now. She had been lucky. The professor had found her, and had offered her the training and education she had needed. She knew there were thousands of others out there who weren't getting the breaks she had recieved. She was determined to help them, at least as much as she could.

The sound of a hard crash echoed through the trees, waking Cyclops from his light sleep. He glanced at her, his powerful energy gaze contained and controlled by the visor covering his eyes.

"What was that?"

"Darned if I know," Storm replied.

They both studied the scope. Two other blips were now stopped where their subject was located, just down the highway. "Seems Sabretooth found a way to stop traffic."

Cyclops laughed. "What traffic? We haven't seen a car in hours."

"Let's go," Storm said.

As they climbed out of the jet, she created a warm breeze around them that held most of the snow back. Better they face whatever was going on fresh and dry and ready to fight.

Within a few seconds they were headed at a fast walk up the road, her breeze and their form-fitting X-Men uniforms keeping them warm and comfortable, despite the subzero temperatures of the Canadian forest.

It wasn't long until they saw exactly what was happening.

As they moved around a slight curve in the road, they could see where a camper had hit a downed tree, smashing the camper and scattering the contents of a trailer it had been pulling. The camper was on fire, with one person trapped inside, on the passenger side of the cab.

Sabretooth was fighting with another man, and as Storm watched, Sabretooth picked the man up and smashed him through the windshield. Judging from the force of the throw, that person was going to be lucky to be alive.

But it was clear the woman in the camper was still alive, and she was struggling to get out—clearly trapped. And now she had a dead weight on top of her.

Side by side, Storm and Cyclops moved up and stood twenty paces behind Sabretooth. The hulking mutant started toward the camper; then he must have sensed them.

He turned, then growled with a low, mean rumble, like an angry animal. He even looked like one, with the skins and long yellow hair.

"Seems we aren't welcome company," Cyclops said.

Sabretooth charged at them, moving quickly on the snow-covered road.

Storm stepped aside as Cyclops fired a hot red beam from his eyes. The beam hit Sabretooth square in the chest.

Hard.

Sabretooth roared as the beam picked him up and flipped him through the air, end over end, smashing through the high branches of the trees and disappearing in a snapping of limbs and brush.

Storm nodded. Their foe wasn't going to be coming back anytime soon.

The only sound now was the crackling of the fire in the camper. Storm ran over to the passenger side, seeing instantly that the intense flames were almost to the camper's propane tank. She kicked up a swirling wind filled with snow and rain to douse the fire, but it wasn't going to work quickly enough. The flames were just too close to the tank and too hot to be put out easily.

Cyclops had also run to the passenger side and yanked open the door.

"Don't touch me!" the girl shouted. "Just help me get the seat loose. I can't move my legs."

Storm focused on the fire, but the propane tank was going to explode, and soon. There wasn't a thing she could do to stop it.

"Cyclops!" Storm said. "Hurry!"

Cyclops focused carefully and used his optic beam to dislodge the seat behind the trapped girl. The seat snapped and came loose.

The girl quickly climbed out and over the hood of the camper, dropping to the ground. At the same time, Storm pulled the unconscious man free.

Suddenly she heard the valve on the propane tank blow off.

It was now or never.

She brought up a massive wind behind them, forcing it in low and hard along the passenger side of the camper. The wind caught her, Cyclops, the girl, and the unconscious man and slid them all down the road on the slick surface, as if they were sliding down a ski slope. All of them were knocked from their feet, and the unconscious guy was rolled like a limp doll. If he wasn't already dead, that hadn't done him any good at all. But Storm hadn't had a choice.

She was just climbing back to her feet when the camper exploded, sending flames and debris into the air, lighting the falling snow with bright orange and yellow colors.

Beside her, the girl and Cyclops stood and stared at the flames. Then the girl said softly, "Thanks."

Chapter Five

Magneto's Headquarters

Mortimer Toynbee laughed when Sabretooth came through the tunnel in the rock and into the laboratory. He was alone.

The lab was a massive space, with towering cliffs of rock, trees, and a giant meadow filled with the machine. Magneto's machine. It sat like a modern statue in the middle of the clearing, its polished metal thrusting toward the invisible roof above. Toynbee had been painting the bottom of the machine, carefully, so as not to miss even the slightest spot.

"Weren't you supposed to bring somebody back with you?" he asked sarcastically. Toynbee was more often called Toad, due largely to his agility, his ability to leap great distances, and his superhuman strength.

Sabretooth paused and turned to face Toad, who only sneered and went back to work. With a growl Sabretooth moved on into Magneto's personal office, through another tunnel in the rock.

Magneto watched him come, shaking his head. Around him the walls of his large office were stark, made of cold, polished stone and metal, just the way he liked it. The space at one time had been a cave, but he'd changed it for his own purposes, placing a massive desk under a single light source, covering the floor with polished tiles.

"My instructions were simple," Magneto said, keeping his voice low and level, not letting his anger seep into the words. "In fact, I made them that way especially for you. And yet you were unable to retrieve our friend."

Sabretooth moved across the room through the shadows and stopped in front of Magneto's desk. The smell of the hides he wore carried over to Magneto, but he ignored it.

"So what happened, brother?"

"Xavier's people," Sabretooth said, his voice low and almost a growl. "They knew."

Magneto nodded and sat back in his chair, musing. Charles was going to be a little harder to beat than he had at first thought.

"Good for you, Charles," Magneto said to himself. "Good for you."

Then Magneto caught a glimpse of the metal dog tags hanging around Sabretooth's neck. He held out his hand, summoning the tags to him.

They snapped off Sabretooth's neck and flew through the air, dropping into his hand. He inspected the tags, staring at the one word at the bottom that didn't seem to belong: *Wolverine*.

"Strange," Magneto said to himself. Then he looked up at Sabretooth. "Where is the mutant now?"

"With Xavier's people," Sabretooth said.

Magneto nodded, tossing the tags across the desk back to Sabretooth.

Then he pushed himself away from the desk, stood, and headed around the desk. "I have made the first move. That is all they know, because that is all you know."

He headed for the door. "Come. We only have three days."

Sabretooth shrugged, grabbed the tags off the desk, and turned to follow.

X-Men Mansion—Westchester County, NY

Logan slowly came back to consciousness, like a swimmer twenty feet down, stroking for the surface of a lake. The light got slowly brighter; then his hearing returned. Then his sense of smell.

He kept his eyes closed, kept his breathing paced, letting his mind clear, giving himself some time. The last thing he could remember was the ugly beast picking him up and tossing him through the window of his truck. The guy had been strong. Very strong. But in a rematch, Logan knew he would get the best of him.

Logan could tell that he was lying on his back on some sort of padded bed in a very sterile place. Some sort of hospital or lab, more than likely. And a very fresh-smelling woman was working nearby.

He let his eyes slit open just a fraction as the woman moved toward him. The room was white and was filled with modern-looking equipment. A box behind her floated off a shelf and came to rest gently in front of her on a tray.

For a moment he was puzzled; then he realized that she was a mutant also.

The woman opened the box and pulled out an IV needle, then turned to him. He kept his eyes in the same position, his breathing consistent, even though her wonderful scent was almost overpowering.

With a gentle touch she picked up his arm, then a moment later he felt the slight prick of the needle. At least she was good at what she did.

Instantly he reacted, sitting up and grabbing her around the throat. The needle broke in his arm, and the box was knocked to the white floor.

For an instant he was unable even to think as he stared into her beautiful face. He couldn't remember ever having this reaction to a woman before. But now was clearly not the time. The way he was holding her, she wouldn't be able to talk, that much was for sure.

She just stared at him, calm and collected, as if his threat meant nothing really. Or as if she was convinced he wasn't going to carry it out.

Disgusted, he let her go, shoving her backward and to the floor. He jumped off the table, realizing he was dressed only in his underwear. And there was something besides his clothes missing: His dog tags were no longer around his neck.

Logan pulled the broken needle from his arm and tossed it at the woman sitting on the floor. She just rubbed her neck and said nothing.

He turned and ran for the nearest door. The sooner he found some clothes and got out of here, the happier he was going to be.

The hallway on the other side of the door was much like the lab he'd just left—sterile, white tiled, and very quiet.

Deathly quiet.

Where the hell was he?

He ran down the hall, away from the lab, letting his full senses bring him information.

The walls were soundproof beyond anything normally done. He couldn't hear anything at all—no sounds of people, machinery, distant traffic, nothing.

The first door he came to was open, so he went through.

It was a fairly large room, also very clean. One side of the room contained lockers, with a padded bench sitting in front of them. The other wall was full of black uniforms hanging side by side, each tagged with a strange "X" insignia.

He quickly rummaged through the lockers, coming up fairly quickly with a pair of pants and a shirt that almost fit.

Behind him in the hallway he could hear the sounds of someone's footsteps. Quickly he finished dressing and headed out another door on the far side. He had no idea how to get out of this place, but if he kept going through doors, eventually he would find the exit.

This door led to another hallway, almost exactly like the first. Logan stopped for an instant, trying to decide which way to go. But then his decision was made for him. A door slid open with the faint *ding* of an elevator. With the footsteps coming across the locker room he'd just left, he dashed into the elevator and let the doors close. The elevator started upward instantly, clearly running automatically.

He got ready to attack whoever might greet him when the elevator door opened, but as it turned out, he didn't need to. The door slid open on a very empty, very plush hallway, exactly the opposite of what he had found below.

He sniffed, taking in the sights and smells. He was clearly in an older mansion, with a large number of people living in it. This hallway was wide and stately, with a high ceiling and expensive furniture along the walls. Plush carpet softened his footsteps, and the smell of furniture polish seemed to dominate.

From down the hall to his right he could hear a voice, so he headed that way, staying to one side and moving silently.

In a moment he could hear exactly what the voice was saying.

"The Roman Empire, for centuries, persecuted and ostracized the Christians, to the extent that they were fed to lions for sport. Then, almost overnight, their religion rose to become the dominant faith in the empire."

"What the hell?" he said softly.

He moved to where the door was slightly ajar and looked through. Inside he could see a strikingly beautiful black woman with pure white hair standing in front of a dozen or so fourteen- to seventeen-year-old children.

Logan studied them, noting that even though they all looked basically normal, it was clear they were all mutants.

An entire class of mutants.

Where was he?

"Does anyone know what caused the Christians to suddenly become accepted?" the woman with the white hair asked her students.

"Yes," one of them said.

The woman nodded for the student to go ahead.

"The emperor suddenly became one," the kid continued.

"That's right," the teacher said. "Which made for some very relieved Christians, I can tell you."

The children all laughed.

Then the woman turned to face the door where Logan was watching through the narrow crack. "Can I help you?"

All the students turned to stare at him.

Logan just shook his head and moved away quickly, heading down the hallway toward a brighter area.

The hallway expanded into a sort of foyer, with a high ceiling and massive antique chandelier. Beside the hall, which led off in both directions, the main way in and out of the foyer was a double oaken door.

Down the hall the elevator he had used *ding*ed faintly again, warning him that someone was coming up—most likely after him.

And from the other direction he could hear the sounds of two people's footsteps on the carpet. He clearly had no choice.

He sprang for the oaken door, opened it silently, and stepped inside, closing it just as silently behind himself.

"Good morning, Logan," a voice said.

Logan spun around and came face-to-face with a middle-aged bald man sitting behind a large mahogany desk. There was a blackboard set up beside the massive desk, and four students were sitting in front of the blackboard, clearly in some sort of class. They all now turned and stared at him.

"Give me a moment, please," the man said to Logan. Then he turned back to his students. "I think that's enough for today, don't you? Off you go."

The four kids all stood and filed past Logan, out the door, looking at him curiously.

Logan didn't know what to do. He knew there were people after him outside that door. Yet this man knew who he was and didn't seem surprised at all that he was here.

Suddenly one of the girls turned back around and ran to the desk. "Forgot my book," she explained.

She grabbed it off the man's desk, then ran for the door.

"Bye, Professor," she said. But the oaken door beside Logan already had been pulled closed. The girl didn't even slow down. Instead she simply ran through the door as if it weren't there.

Logan stared at the hard wood where she had disappeared, then back at the man she had called "Professor."

The man held up a textbook as if it explained everything. "Physics," he said. Then, "Would you like some breakfast?"

Logan just stared at him. He had been prepared to fight his way out, not to be offered something to eat. What the hell was going on here? He needed some answers, and he needed them fast.

"Where am I?" he demanded.

"Westchester, New York," the man said. "You were attacked. My people brought you here for medical attention."

"I don't need medical attention," Logan said. He was still hurting slightly in a half dozen places, but he certainly wasn't going to admit it to this guy.

The man smiled. "Yes, of course."

The man turned and wheeled himself out from

behind his desk. For the first time Logan realized the man was confined to a wheelchair.

The bald-headed guy moved toward Logan, extending his hand. "I'm sorry. Let me introduce myself. I'm Professor Charles Xavier. You're at my school for gifted children. Actually, mutants, as the press calls us. You'll be safe here from Magneto."

Logan shook the man's hand, then, puzzled, he asked, "What's a magneto?"

The professor chuckled. "A very powerful mutant who believes that there is a war brewing between us and the rest of humanity."

"So?" Logan asked, glaring at the professor. "What does that have to do with me?"

"I don't know yet," the professor admitted. "I wish I did. But I believe Magneto is planning some kind of preemptive strike. I've been following his actions for some time. The mutant that attacked you is an associate of Magneto's called Sabretooth."

"You knew he was going to attack me?"

The professor shook his head. "No, I just tracked Sabretooth, and he led my people to you. We need to keep you out of Magneto's reach until we know what his interest is."

At that, Logan decided he had had enough. "Sorry, pal. I've got to get back to my—" Suddenly he realized he didn't have any idea where his camper and belongings were.

"Sorry," the professor said. "It's gone."

Logan stared at him. The guy couldn't mean his camper. Granted he had smashed it up pretty badly, but it still had to be somewhere.

"Your truck was destroyed," the professor said. "A fire started in the collision and ignited the propane tank. We barely got you out in time. There was nothing left."

Logan said nothing.

"Logan, it's been almost fifteen years, hasn't it? Since you woke up?"

Logan wanted to turn and run, but he didn't.

"Woke up?"

"Woke up," the professor said, "with no knowledge of who you really are. Living day to day, trying to piece together what happened to you. You know how to fight, though. You always have known, haven't you? And your nightmares are vague clues to a past that isn't completely erased from your mind. But now that everything has been destroyed, where will you go?"

"How—?" Logan asked. "How did you know all that?"

You're not the only one with gifts, the professor said. It took Logan a moment to realize that the professor's lips hadn't moved at all.

Behind him the door opened, and three others came in, with Rogue, the girl who had been in his truck with him. One was the black woman who had been teaching the kids, the other was a guy with strange-looking sunglasses, and the third was the beautiful woman from the lab.

"Ah, thank you," the professor said aloud. "Dr. Grey, allow me to introduce Logan."

The beautiful woman from the lab, the one he had choked in his escape, smiled pleasantly and stepped forward, her hand extended. "Yes, we've met. Call me Jean."

Logan looked into her eyes as he took her hand. In all his life he had never seen a woman so beautiful. Or one to whom he had been so attracted. Her hand was soft, yet strong in his. Her grip was firm. And he didn't want to let go.

Professor Xavier continued with the introductions. "This is Scott Summers, also called Cyclops. Ororo Munroe, also called Storm. They are the ones who saved your life."

Logan glanced at them, but he turned his attention to the young Rogue and said nothing.

"Don't mention it," Cyclops said.

Logan noticed that Dr. Grey put her hand on the Cyclops guy's arm. It was clearly the action of a girl-friend. Subtle, but not something Logan would miss. He wasn't going to like this Cyclops, he knew right away.

"What are you going to do with her?" Logan asked, moving closer to Rogue, but careful not to touch her.

The professor smiled at Rogue with real warmth. And in that smile Logan saw a clear expression of understanding. "Rogue's been on her own now for some time, searching for a home. A place to belong."

Rogue nodded, clearly happy to be here. And that was all fine and good, as far as Logan was concerned.

Xavier turned back to face Logan. "We're going to give her that."

Rogue nodded, confirming what was clear to Logan.

"So," Logan said, glancing at the others, "this place is sort of a dog pound for unwanted mutants, is that it?"

"It's a school," the professor said calmly.

Logan shrugged. "I don't really believe what you're

doing here, but, lucky for me, I don't care." He started for the door. "Thanks for the ride."

"Hold on," the Cyclops guy said, stepping toward him.

That was when the anger Logan felt, toward the guy they called Sabretooth, about losing his camper, all came boiling up at once. He felt as though he just had to take it out on someone, and the guy with the sunglasses seemed like the perfect target.

Without hesitation, Logan slugged the guy, knocking him back into the wall.

Cyclops hit hard, one hand blocking his fall while the other shot up as he checked to make sure his sunglasses were still in place. *Vain dude,* Logan thought contemptuously.

Cyclops scrambled to his feet, clearly angry.

Logan was impressed. This guy could take a punch.

Cyclops started back toward Logan, but Logan stood his ground, just hoping the guy would charge. He really needed to pound on someone right now.

"Cyclops!" Jean said in a crisp, loud voice.

Logan's claws came out as the kid kept coming.

"Logan, stop!" Jean said. "Please?"

She stepped between Cyclops and Logan, moving toward Logan, right at his extended claws.

"Jean!" Cyclops said.

Storm stepped forward and stopped the sunglass kid before he could move any farther. Smart of her, as far as Logan was concerned.

Logan kept his claws extended, and Jean, her beautiful eyes staring straight into his, stopped right as their tips nudged her throat. He had to admit, she was brave.

"I know you think none of this is your concern,"

Jean said. "But Magneto will find you. And a lot of lives could be in danger, including your own."

He slowly retracted his claws, but he didn't turn away from her calm, deep gaze. He could stare into her eyes forever, as far as he was concerned.

Then Xavier stepped in.

"Logan, I'll make you a deal," he said. "You give me forty-eight hours to figure out what Magneto wants with you, and I will give you my word that, no matter what happens, I'll use all my power to help you piece together what you've lost. And what you're looking for."

Logan, still staring at Jean, nodded. His claws finished retracting, his fists opened, and his shoulders relaxed. "Forty-eight hours, old man," he said. "Cross me, and I won't feel any guilt about what I do."

Jean smiled. "Thank you, Logan."

At that he could say nothing.

Chapter Six

Washington, DC

Senator Kelly smiled and clapped his heavy hands together as the limousine pulled onto the tarmac of the airport. "Looks like we have some supporters."

Henry Guyrich, his aide, nodded, but he wasn't really looking at the supporters, or at Kelly. Kelly didn't really care what Guyrich thought. Or, for that matter, what anyone thought—except for the pollsters. And right now, the polls showed that his antimutant stance was getting him a lot of attention, perhaps even votes. And he was going to keep riding the issue until it no longer yielded those benefits.

The limo came to a stop beside a large government helicopter, the pilot already waiting in his seat. The path between the limo and the helicopter was lined by a cheering crowd, barely restrained by a short rope.

Senator Kelly stepped out into the cold and pulled his overcoat tighter around his stomach, then turned toward the crowd, waving and smiling. He could see there were at least two hundred people there, many brandishing antimutant signs. One even had a stuffed mutant hanging from a pole. A few reporters had cameras set up and were doing a live remote.

He moved along the crowd, shaking hands, smiling, giving the thumbs-up signal that was becoming his trademark. Around him the crowd cheered even more enthusiastically, encouraging him to keep going, to stop those mutants. He loved this attention. He could feel it fueling him, giving him the extra strength he needed to keep going.

He finally reached the bottom of the stairs that led up into the helicopter. He climbed three steps, then again paused and waved, making sure the cameras had time to catch him fully. Then, with one last quick thumbs-up, he moved inside.

Behind him his aide, Guyrich, followed carrying the senator's briefcase. As he climbed aboard, he glanced toward the pilot, who nodded in acknowledgment.

No one noticed anything out of the ordinary. Not even the senator.

X-Men Mansion

The bright winter sun flooded the large solarium, warming the air around the students and Storm. Rogue sat near the back, a pile of books on the floor beside her, watching as Storm lectured.

This was all so new to her. She had never expected to be included in a class again after what had happened in her old school. Yet here she was, with people who knew what she could do and didn't care. It was going to take her some time to get used to that.

She also had new clothes that fit over a very light

body stocking that had been provided to keep anyone from accidentally touching her. It was wonderfully soft and comfortable.

Storm stood in front of them, her skin almost radiant in the sunlight, her white hair flowing like a waterfall around her head. She and Dr. Grey were the most beautiful women Rogue had ever seen. Someday, she wanted to be like them. She had already decided that.

"So, the barometric pressure begins to drop," Storm was saying. "Precipitation begins, and the air starts to move more rapidly. Now lightning strikes occur when strong thermal updrafts cause water droplets and ice crystals to collide, creating positively and negatively charged particles."

A student named Frederick, who sat in front, raised his hand.

"Yes?" Storm said.

"Are you sure about this?" Frederick asked, smiling.

"Don't tempt me to demonstrate," she said, shaking her head with a hint of amusement. Then she turned back to the board.

Rogue smiled at another boy who sat in front of her. His name was John. He was the cutest boy she had seen in a long, long time.

Kitty, who was sitting beside Rogue, whispered. "So, that guy you came in with? He's really got steel claws that come out of his hands?"

Jubilee, who was sitting on the other side of Rogue, whispered back. "No way. What kind of mutation is that?"

Rogue just shrugged, watching John as he pulled out a lighter and clicked it. Then he held his hand under the flame and pulled the lighter away, keeping the flame in place, hovering over his hand.

Despite all that she had experienced, Rogue was astonished.

He just smiled, and the flame grew into a ball the size of an orange.

"Showing off again," Jubilee said, shaking her head, but John ignored her.

Now the fireball over John's hand was even bigger, almost the size of a grapefruit. Then suddenly the flame was engulfed in a ball of ice. Glancing around, Rogue found another student—Bobby—holding out a crystal rose for her. Though beautiful, it was already beginning to melt.

Then Rogue glanced at Storm. She didn't look happy.

"John, what did I tell you?" Storm asked, frowning.

"Sorry," John said.

Storm shook her head, then turned to finish what she was writing on the board.

John glanced back and smiled at Rogue. Right then and there, she knew she was really going to like this place.

Twenty minutes later the class ended. Rogue picked up her books, watching as the other students left, some stopping to talk to Storm about some topic.

Bobby took his time, until Jubilee and Kitty had moved off, then smiled again at Rogue. "You want to meet me for dinner?" he asked. "I'll show you around."

Rogue could feel her heart jump. She was flattered and scared at the same time. "Okay, sure."

"Great!" he said. He headed for the door with a happy, "See ya."

Rogue finished picking up her books as Storm moved toward her. "So, how are you doing?"

Rogue looked around in wonder, at the glass-walled room and winter gardens beyond. "This place is so beautiful. And everyone is so nice. I just—"

She didn't know what to say, so she just stopped.

Storm nodded. "How long have you been on your own?"

Rogue stared into the eyes of the beautiful teacher. "Eight months. I've just been hitchhiking, trying to get as far away from home as possible. Get away from anyone who would know what I was."

Storm nodded. "That I understand."

"I didn't know there was anyplace for us to go," Rogue said. "But this is wonderful. I've felt kind of alone, you know."

"Well," Storm said, "you're not alone anymore."

"And the professor?" Rogue said, looking into Storm's eyes. "He can actually cure me?"

Rogue watched with surprise as the smile suddenly drained from her teacher's face. After a few seconds, Storm sat down in a chair and motioned for Rogue to sit across from her.

There, over the next hour, Rogue learned things she didn't want to know. And understood that maybe she would never, ever be able to touch another person again, as long as she lived.

And that no one would ever touch or kiss her in return.

Suddenly she felt even more alone than she had on the road.

Chapter Seven

X-Men Mansion

Logan was getting the official tour from Professor Xavier himself. He wasn't sure why the old guy was spending the time with him, but whatever the reason, Logan figured to be gone in less than forty-eight hours, so it didn't matter in the slightest.

Logan walked slowly, pacing the professor's wheelchair as it moved silently along the floor. They were in a wing of the mansion that Logan hadn't seen before. The place was massive. He had already been shown a huge solarium and more rooms than he could count. And everything was distinctly first-class. Clearly there was some money behind all this.

Of course, if the professor could read minds—as it seemed he could—there certainly wouldn't be a problem getting money.

"The dining rooms, kitchen, and parlor are found in the other wing," the professor said, going on with the tour. "As you can see, everything on this floor and above has been designed to be viewed by the general public. As far as they know, this is merely a school for 'gifted' students."

The professor led Logan to a panel in the wall and stopped. A hidden elevator door opened with a *ping*, and they got inside.

"The subbasements however, are an entirely different matter."

"So how'd I get in here?" Logan asked. "You didn't bring me in through the front door."

The door of the elevator opened, revealing the lab corridor that Logan had run down during his attempted escape.

"Come on," the professor said. "I'll show you."

They moved down the corridor, turning twice before reaching wide doors that opened automatically onto a massive hangar. It was bigger than anything Logan would have imagined. More than likely it could hold an airliner or two. But at the moment, it seemed to be primarily dedicated to a modernistic, shiny black jet like none that Logan had ever seen.

"Vertical takeoff and landings," the professor said, motioning toward the jet. "Instruments that allow it to fly in any weather."

"Amazing," Logan said, moving out into the hangar and looking around curiously. He pointed to the large doors at the end. "Hidden entrance?"

The professor nodded. "Perfectly hidden."

"So why all this?" Logan asked, motioning at the equipment and the jet.

"Everyone here has abilities," Xavier said. "Powers. Curses, until they can be controlled. All of us have hurt and been hurt. And none of us asked to be the way we are."

"I hear you there," Logan said.

"When I was fifteen years old," the professor said, "I began to hear people's thoughts. At first I thought I was going mad. One day I read the mind of one of my teachers and saw that he was going to fail me, simply because he didn't like me."

"I bet that pissed you off," Logan said.

"It did at that," the professor commented. "I was so mad I put a suggestion in his mind that he was having a heart attack. He nearly died."

Logan looked down at the old man with a little more respect. It hadn't dawned on him that reading someone's mind could have other uses. Dangerous uses, it seemed. "So what'd you do?"

"I was terrified," the professor said, "as most everyone here was when something first happened to them. I withdrew from everything, fearful that I might hurt someone else. I thought I was alone."

"But you weren't."

The professor nodded slightly. "That was when I met Eric Lehnsherr. Eric, too, had a power. He could create magnetic fields, enabling him to manipulate metal. He helped me understand what I was. And to find ways of controlling my power. Eric also showed me that there were others like us."

"How long ago was this?" Logan asked.

The professor smiled. "More years ago than I care to think about. As the years went by and our numbers increased, so did the prejudice and fear of ordinary humans. Our world changed, and Eric changed with it. He believed that humanity would never accept us, that a war between mutants and humans was inevitable. He was angry, vengeful. That's when he became Magneto."

"And you could no longer stay with him?" Logan asked.

"Exactly," the professor said, clearly still sad about it despite all the years. He moved on, toward the stables and the garage. "I opened this school, a place where mutants could be safe from persecution. This is a place where they could not only learn to focus their powers, but also learn that mankind is not evil. Just uninformed."

"You still didn't answer my question," Logan said. "Why all this hardware?"

The professor continued. "There are mutants out there with incredible power, Logan. I knew that a day would come when some of them might use that power against the rest of humanity. And that if there was no one to challenge them, humanity's days would end."

"So you are the challenge," Logan said, nodding.

"Evil men succeed when good men do nothing," the professor said. "A famous quote that Eric taught me once."

Logan nodded again. This was a much, much bigger operation than he had first thought. It was going to be great to get out of here and let them fight all their good fights for as long as they wanted.

"Now," Professor Xavier said, turning his chair back toward the hallway. "If you wouldn't mind, Dr. Grey would like to examine you."

Logan laughed. Having Dr. Grey do anything to him was just about his idea of heaven.

The East Coast—Above Washington, DC

Senator Kelly hung up the phone and sat back in the soft chair of the helicopter, staring out the window at the ground flashing past. The drone of the motors faded to background noise in the extraordinarily luxurious interior. Kelly loved traveling like this. He considered it one of the God-given rights of his job. And he used his rights as often as he felt he needed, which was often.

He stared at the phone. That call with the president had gone almost exactly as he had expected. Sometimes things went well, sometimes they went poorly, and other times they just didn't go at all.

"Well," Guyrich said, "what was his opinion?"

Kelly shrugged and leaned forward to pour himself another glass of scotch. "He's the president of the United States. He doesn't have an opinion. He smiles, he waves, he shakes hands."

"Isn't that what you do, sir?" Guyrich asked.

Kelly shot his aide a sharp look across the table, then put the scotch bottle back between them. Guyrich had been acting strange lately. If he didn't shape up, Kelly would have to have a talk with him about his attitude. The last thing Kelly needed right now was a problem with his staff.

"Well," Kelly said, leaning back and sipping, enjoying the smooth taste of the expensive scotch, "this time it's not up to him. It's up to me and Congress."

"Have you thought about a demonstration of some kind?" Guyrich asked. "Maybe use the UN Summit to our advantage. The whole world will be watching."

"I'm only interested in Americans," Kelly said, his voice harsher than he intended. He caught himself. "Let the rest of the world deal with mutants in any damn way they please. Besides, only Americans can vote for me."

He laughed and took another sip, then decided to go on. "This is the sort of problem that liberals just beg you to ignore, until it crawls up and bites them on the tail. And guys like us are left to clean it up."

He stared into the eyes of his aide. "You know, this situation, these mutants, are the reason people like me exist."

Kelly glanced out the window as the helicopter crossed out over the cold, dark gray waters of the Atlantic. They weren't supposed to be over water on this flight, especially not the ocean.

"Hey, where the hell are we?"

Kelly glanced back at his aide, waiting for an answer. Instead he witnessed a horror story. Right before his eyes, Guyrich was changing. His face was shifting, his clothes seeming to draw inward, until finally, where Guyrich had been sitting, Kelly found a beautiful woman covered completely in iridescent blue scales. She had solid yellow eyes that made her look more like a cat than a human.

She just smiled, and said nothing.

It took a moment for Senator Kelly's mind to register what he had just seen. Then he realized that he was facing a mutant. A mutant who had been posing as his aide.

Instantly he jumped for the cockpit door.

But the blue woman was faster. A *lot* faster. As he moved past her, she planted a solid kick to his stomach.

The air rushed out and he doubled over, sliding toward the door. As quick as he could, he climbed back to his feet and yanked open the cockpit door.

"Pilot! Help!"

The pilot leered at him through grotesque features. A long tongue flicked briefly at him.

The copilot seat was empty.

It shouldn't be empty, he thought frantically. *There are always two pilots on these flights.*

Kelly turned back to the blue woman, who was standing behind him.

She took a step toward him, and he swung at her. He wasn't going to let any damned mutant take him without a fight.

It was as if he were moving in slow motion. She caught his hand and hit him five or six times with kicks and punches before he could even fall down.

He coughed, trying to catch his breath as he lay face-down on the carpet-covered floor. Suddenly strong hands grabbed him and flipped him over on his back. The blue face and yellow eyes came right down over him like a nightmare that he couldn't seem to wake up from.

"You know," the blue woman said, "people like you are the reason I was afraid to go to school as a child."

She stood and kicked him solidly in his stomach, forcing what little was left of his breath out of him.

He worked to breathe, choking and coughing as he stared up at her through water-filled eyes.

She started to turn away, then, almost as an after-thought, she raised a foot and brought it down solidly on the side of his head.

Merciful blackness took him almost instantly.

It would be hours before he awoke. And then he would be very sorry he did.

Chapter
Eight

X-Men Mansion

Jean leaned against the edge of the doorway of Logan's room and watched, smiling, as he took down the pictures from the walls and put them in drawers. The two of them had talked off and on, through his medical examination and then through the entire dinner. She had then offered to show him his room, and he had gladly accepted. Any excuse to spend more time with Dr. Jean Grey was just fine with him.

"So why do so many mutants end up coming through here?" Logan asked as he slammed a drawer shut.

"Most mutants leave pretty ugly situations behind them," Jean said. "People find out what you are, so a lot of mutants have to start out with a new identity. We not only help them with their control of their powers, we help them with the new identities and starting new lives, as well."

Logan nodded, sorting through the clothes someone had put on his bed. They all looked as if they would fit, but some he just wouldn't be caught dead in.

"So," Logan said, turning to face her. "You move things with your mind?"

"It's called telekinesis," she said.

"Right," Logan said. "You move stuff with your mind. Anything else?"

"I also have some telepathic abilities."

Logan stared at her suspiciously. "You mean like the professor?"

She shook her head. "My telepathy is nowhere near as powerful as Professor Xavier's. But sometimes, if I make a strong connection."

"So," Logan said, noting her obvious discomfort as she revealed things about herself. "Why are you just plain old Jean Grey?"

"What do you mean?"

"You couldn't think of some cute mutant nickname? Seems that just about everyone else has one."

She laughed. "Honestly, I haven't chosen one yet."

He pushed the pile of clothes he liked into the middle of the bed and sat down, feeling the unaccustomed softness under him. "How about Mrs. Cyclops. You guys are a couple, right?"

Again, she laughed and nodded.

"He seems kinda tense," Logan commented, "for a woman like you."

"Oh," she said, smiling, "is that so?"

"Seems that way to me," Logan said.

"When Professor Xavier found Scott, he hadn't opened his eyes in two months. Awake, asleep, not at all in two months."

"Why?" Logan asked. "Didn't like what he was seeing?"

"No," Jean said. "Even with his visor, it's very hard for him to control the energy that comes from his eyes. Without the visor, if he opened his eyes, he could easily punch through a mountain as simply as you could crush a beer can. He has to be in control every minute of every day."

Logan nodded. She and the professor had been right. Everyone here had a curse of one sort or another. He stared at her as the silence between them grew slightly uncomfortable. On the perfect skin of her neck he could see the bruises left from where he had grabbed her earlier.

"Sorry about that," he said.

"Sorry about what?"

He shrugged. "If I hurt you. Earlier. Sorry."

She paused, smiling, and reached out to touch him. As she did, her head jerked back, her face pale. There had been a clear connection between them for a moment there, albeit an unexpected one. Clearly she had gotten something from his mind.

"What did you see?" He fought to keep from reacting to the unexpected intrusion.

She took a deep breath and let it slowly out. What she had seen had shocked her in some fashion or another. He waited until she gathered herself.

Finally she said, "Just images. And pain. Lots of pain. What happened to you?"

"Bad things, darlin'," he said. "Bad things."

"Don't you think it's past your bedtime, Logan?" Cyclops said as he stepped into the doorway and stood beside Jean. "Or do you want Jean to tell you a story?"

Logan snorted. "I bet she's got a few you haven't heard."

Jean sighed and shot Cyclops a look of frustration. "Let me know when you two start butting antlers. I'll get my camera."

She turned and left, clearly flustered by what she had seen in Logan's mind. And, Logan guessed, because Cyclops had stuck his nose in where it didn't belong.

Logan stared at Cyclops and, despite the visor, it was plain he was staring back.

"You gonna tell me to stay away from your girl?" Logan asked, sneering at Cyclops.

"If I had to do that," Cyclops said, "she wouldn't be my girl."

Cyclops stepped into the room. Logan stayed on the bed, not moving, but ready to if something warranted it.

"Rogue said you were like an animal in that bar," Cyclops said. "I think she meant it as a compliment. She was very impressed. But fighting humans is very different from taking on mutants. Especially Magneto."

"You've fought him, have you?" Logan asked.

"We haven't had to resort to that," Cyclops said. "Yet."

Logan laughed. "You're prepping for a war, and I'm not convinced you could handle yourself in a heated discussion. I'm guessing I'm the only one here who's seen any real combat."

"And when was that?" Cyclops asked.

Logan just stared. He wasn't about to go over what little he remembered with this wet-nosed kid. "Previously."

"Don't like to talk about your past, huh?"

"Got it in one," Logan said. "Especially to you."

"It just must kill you that I saved your life," Cyclops said.

Logan only snorted. He actually hadn't given it much thought, but he wasn't going to bait the kid with that.

Cyclops laughed. "Don't worry. It won't happen again."

Logan only shrugged.

Cyclops turned and headed for the door. There he stopped and looked back. "And Logan," Cyclops said, his face hard and very intense. "Stay away from my girl."

With that Cyclops moved off down the hall, leaving Logan to sit on his bed and smile.

Jean Grey stood in the laboratory in front of the light board, staring at the X rays posted there. To one side sat Professor Xavier, and behind him stood Cyclops and Storm. All of them were in their comfortable clothes. Storm had even had to get dressed to come down, because this gathering was later than normal.

But when Jean had left Logan, she had still been too wired to sleep, so she'd gone back to her lab to finish reviewing his physical exam results. What she had found had caused her to call the others immediately.

While they were on the way, she had taken the time to gather herself, calm herself. She didn't want to admit—or show—how much that flash of mental contact had bothered her. Especially to Scott. He was having enough trouble with her even talking to Logan.

The X rays on the light board showed different angles of Logan's skeleton, from the skull down to his fingers and toes. It looked more like a creation of a Deco architect than something natural, that was for sure. Much of the skeleton was streamlined, refined in many strange ways. Clearly manufactured.

And the claws running from the back of his arms down to his knuckles looked downright mean. The design was brilliant, allowing them to work based purely on muscle control.

Even after an hour of studying the X rays, she still couldn't believe what she was seeing. When the others arrived, she started by pointing out the bones, bright white on the X ray, then glanced at the professor. "The metal is an alloy called adamantium."

"You're kidding," Cyclops said.

"I didn't think that was possible," the professor said, staring at the X rays, his features calm as always.

"I didn't either," Jean said. "Until today, I thought adamantium to be a myth. Impenetrable, unbreakable. Supposedly indestructible." She pointed at the white on the X rays. "But all that is adamantium."

"How in the world did anyone even work it into shapes?" Storm asked.

Jean just shook her head. "I've no idea. But it's been surgically grafted to his entire skeleton. Even around his joints and over his skull."

"Amazing," Cyclops said.

"How could he have survived a procedure like that?" Storm asked.

"His mutation," Jean said, glancing at the professor to make sure she was on the right track. "Logan has uncharted regenerative capability, which enables him to heal rapidly. This also makes his age impossible to determine. For all we know, he could very well be older than you, Professor."

Xavier smiled.

Cyclops laughed, then asked, "Any idea who did this to him? Or why?"

The professor was about to answer, but Jean jumped in ahead of him, basing her answer on her last conversation with Logan, and the mental connection they had shared. "He doesn't know. Nor does he remember anything about his life before the operation happened. But he remembers the pain."

Professor Xavier stared at her for a moment, clearly surprised that she knew what she did. Then he sighed. "This is something I've feared all along: experimentation on mutants. It's not entirely unheard-of, but I've never seen anything like this before."

The idea that Logan had been the subject of someone's inhuman experiment upset Jean more than she wanted to admit.

"So," Cyclops said, staring at Jean for an instant before glancing at the professor, "what do you think Magneto wants with him?"

The professor pointed at the X rays on the wall. "I'm not entirely sure it's *him* that Magneto wants."

"The adamantium?" Storm asked.

The professor didn't answer.

Jean knew he didn't have to.

Chapter Nine

X-Men Mansion

Jean slowly, and as quietly as she could, went about her normal bedtime routine. As always this late at night, the mansion around her was quiet.

Scott was already in bed, lying on his back as he always did, his visor secured to the back of his head so that it wouldn't accidentally come off in his sleep.

She couldn't tell if he was sleeping or not, so she simply slipped into bed beside him and turned off the lights. It had been a very strange day. Much had changed. And she was still unsettled with her glimpse into Logan's mind, and worried about Scott's jealousy of him. That wasn't like Scott at all.

In the dark, Scott's visor was glowing softly. It dimmed slightly once when he blinked. He was awake.

"What's wrong?" she asked.

"I hate him," Scott said.

"Why?" Jean asked, startled at Scott's blunt reply.

"The way he looks at you," Scott said. "His eyes. I just don't trust him."

She smiled and curled up against him, putting her head on his chest. "You know I love you, Scott," she said. "And you should trust me."

She kissed him, and after that, there just wasn't much to be said.

Outside, in the hallway, Rogue walked quietly, trying not to wake anyone. She had on her nightgown and the body stocking that protected others from her.

She had tossed and turned for the past hour, thinking about the day, worrying about the future and what Storm had told her.

There was no cure for being a mutant. Her only options were acceptance and control.

She had so wanted a cure.

She had held out hope since leaving home that she someday might find one.

That dream had been shattered, and she was more afraid than she had ever been, even when on the road with the truckers. But now she was afraid of the future, of what it held for her.

Rogue reached Logan's door and slowly opened it, peeking inside.

"Logan?" she said softly.

No response.

She moved inside and closed the door behind her, staring at him. He was sleeping fitfully, grunting and talking some in his sleep. She couldn't understand what he was saying.

She watched him for a moment, then moved over to the big round chair near his bed. There, in the chair, she curled up and closed her eyes.

Just being close to him made her feel safe.

After a few moments, she too was asleep.

Magneto's Headquarters

Senator Kelly slowly came to, the pain in his head a pounding drum, throbbing with each beat of his heart. At first he couldn't remember what had happened. Nothing around him, from the trees to the clearing floor and rock cliffs, looked familiar.

When he tried to touch his head, he discovered his hands were tied behind his back. He was bound to a metal chair.

He looked down slowly, so as not to increase his headache, trying to focus his eyes. He could tell that he was still dressed in his suit and tie. Maybe he was being robbed? No, that didn't make sense, since he could still feel his wallet in his back pocket.

Slowly but surely, the memory came back, like a bad dream drifting in over the pain: Guyrich turning into a blue mutant. The blue woman had beat him, kicked him in the head.

The memory sent a sharp stab shooting through his skull.

Had it really happened?

His vision slowly cleared a little more, so that he could focus over the throbbing ache. He let himself move his pounding head slowly, looking for anything around him that just might seem familiar.

Most of the space that surrounded him was shaded in darkness. It was a clearing of some sort, inside a covered place. There were trees and rocks and massive stone walls with arching metal entrances. The sound of running water was a continuous background noise. The air was warm, and there was almost no breeze. He could smell a faint aroma of pine and ocean salt.

He had never seen anyplace like this before. Fantastic architecture blended right in with the forest and rocks, as if the two belonged together, yet it was clear that the man-made features were dominant.

Then Kelly noticed a heavy man standing on one side of the clearing, just in the shadows, staring up into a tree. A bird was chirping there, jumping from limb to limb. The man watched intently until something shot out of his mouth and grabbed the bird, pulling it right out of the tree.

Kelly stared, not believing what he was seeing. It was the man's tongue stuck to the bird.

One very *long* tongue.

The bird struggled but couldn't get loose. The guy's mouth opened extra wide, as if his jaws had come unhinged, and he took in the entire bird. Then, with his eyes closed as if savoring a special treat, the man chewed up the bird, eating it alive, bones and all. Senator Kelly could hear the smacking and cracking sounds even from where he sat.

He wanted to be sick. He turned away as much as he could, closed his eyes, working to keep his empty stomach from pushing up through his throat. Never in all of his life had he seen such a perverted act.

He struggled with his bindings, fighting to get loose. He had to get out of here, wherever here was.

Slowly another man—a powerful-looking, stately man—emerged from one of the tubelike entrances in the cliff wall and moved into the light. He smiled at Kelly.

"Who are you?" the senator demanded. "Where is my aide? Why have you taken me?"

"My name is Magneto, Senator Kelly," the man said, his voice rich and deep and in control, with just a hint of an accent. "Your aide, Mr. Guyrich, has been dead for some time. But I've had Mystique here keep you company."

The blue woman stepped out of the shadows and wrapped her arms around Magneto, as a lover might, claiming territory.

Kelly pushed back, wanting to get as far away from her as he could. But his bonds wouldn't allow him to move at all, and the chair was far, far too heavy to push. So instead he decided to confront this Magneto.

"You know, don't you," Kelly said, "that whatever you do to me will just prove me right? Every word I've spoken will be confirmed."

Magneto laughed, letting Mystique slip off and step back. "Gosh, I sure hope so."

That wasn't the answer Kelly had expected. He watched as the man stepped closer. He didn't look dangerous. Not like the blue woman. But with mutants there was no way of telling. And with a name like Magneto, he had to be a mutant.

"Are you a God-fearing man, Senator?"

Kelly pushed back, trying everything he could to get away from the man who just kept getting closer and closer.

Magneto laughed. "Seems you are certainly afraid of something at the moment. But God-fearing man? Such a strange phrase, don't you think?"

Kelly said nothing, trying to catch his breath as Magneto went on. The throbbing in his head increased.

"I've always thought of God as a teacher. As a bringer of light, wisdom, and understanding."

To his own surprise, Kelly found it was everything he could do to keep from screaming. The man had moved even closer and was almost leaning down in front of him. In the background, the man who ate birds and the blue woman stood, watching, smiling. They were clearly enjoying what Magneto was doing to him.

"You see," Magneto said, coming right up into Kelly's face, "I think what you really are afraid of is me. Me and my kind, the brotherhood of mutants."

Kelly's head felt as if it were going to explode. His entire body was shaking with fear.

Magneto smiled, looking Kelly right in the eyes for the longest time. Then, without blinking, he stood, turned, and walked away.

Suddenly Kelly's chair moved, clearly being dragged along the ground behind Magneto by some unseen force.

"Oh, fearing mutants is not surprising, really," Magneto said as he walked, talking as if he and Kelly were just engaging in a normal conversation while they strolled in a forest. Only Kelly wasn't walking.

"As a friend has pointed out to me often," Magneto continued, "humans have always feared what they don't understand. True?"

Magneto glanced back at Kelly, but Kelly stubbornly refused to give the mutant the pleasure of an answer. So Magneto went on, talking and walking, with Kelly's chair bumping along the ground behind him.

"And mankind has always made laws to protect itself from what it doesn't understand. Laws like your mutant registration law."

"The intention of the Mutant Registration Act—"

Magneto stopped and turned on Kelly, cutting him off in midsentence. Kelly's chair slammed to a stop.

"Intention?" Magneto's eyes flashed with some sort of inner pain, and his voice rose almost to a shout. He calmed quickly. "Senator, you and I both know all about the road to hell and what it is paved with."

Kelly said nothing, but he didn't look away.

"We are not talking about intentions, Senator. We are talking about mankind. Human fear. And trust me when I tell you, it is only a matter of time before mutants will be herded into camps, studied for weaknesses, and eventually wiped off the face of the Earth."

Magneto pointed to the faint blue numbers tattooed into the inside of his arm. Nazi prison camp tattoos. Despite himself, Kelly was shocked.

"Trust me, Senator. I know," Magneto said. "I've seen it happen in my lifetime."

Kelly shook his head. There was nothing he could say. Nothing he dared say at this point.

Magneto shrugged and turned. "Well, I'm much more giving than that. I simply want to show you, to help you understand."

Magneto waved his hand, and the entire area lit up. It became clear that Kelly was in a forest clearing, with towering cliff walls all around. Something stretched overhead, from cliff wall to cliff wall, enclosing the clearing, but Kelly couldn't see what it was.

Stonework and metal structures blended into the cliff walls, almost as if they had been formed there. Tunnel openings disappeared into the cliffs in a number of different places. Every line was flowing, yet everything seemed stark and oversized.

The center of the clearing drew Kelly's attention.

A machine?

A sculpture?

Kelly wasn't sure. The metal seemed to flow upward from a round base supporting three pillars that held up a platform forty feet in the air. On the platform sat two curved, almost tusk-shaped metal spires, arcing into the air twenty feet above, pointing at each other but not touching. It all appeared to be made of metal, and it seemed to shine under its own power.

It was the most fantastic thing, sculpture or machine, that Kelly had ever seen.

Magneto walked toward it, still talking. "Don't fear God, Senator. And certainly, most certainly, don't fear me." Magneto laughed. Then he added, "At least not anymore."

"What is it you intend to do to me?" Kelly shouted at Magneto's back.

"Let's just say that God works too slowly," Magneto said as he stepped up onto the base of the sculpture.

Suddenly Kelly realized that his first impression had been right. It wasn't a sculpture, but instead some incredible machine.

Magneto stood facing Kelly, his feet apart. He placed his hands on two upright posts.

Magneto jerked as his hands seemed to be yanked solidly against the posts; then he was whisked up the center to the top of the machine, where he was locked into place under the two curving metal shapes.

A set of metal rings rose up around Magneto, spinning slowly at first, then faster and faster.

The air around Kelly seemed to be charged with energy; the light seemed brighter. A slight wind started to blow, swirling around Kelly.

Everything gained in intensity as the rings moved faster and faster, forming a blur around the mutant.

Then the air started to ripple off the machine, like waves on clear water.

Kelly wanted to look away, but he couldn't. Energy seemed to pour from Magneto's hands, through the post and into the rings swirling around him.

The rings were now moving so fast that they weren't even a blur, but instead formed a ball. The air around the machine was rippling away harder and harder. Magneto had his eyes closed. He was straining with all his might to do what he was doing.

Then the rings began to glow.

Dull red at first, then brighter and brighter, until they became almost a white ball around the mutant. Kelly wanted to shade his eyes, but his hands were tied. He turned his head, the headache growing again from the intense light.

Magneto was barely visible behind the light. Nonetheless, the strain was very evident on his face.

Where before it had been silent, now a whine came from the machine. It started to grow. The light coming off the rings vanished. Yet Kelly could still see the faint outline of the ball that showed the incredibly fast rings.

Louder and louder the whine cut through the vast chamber.

The sound filled the space, bounced off the cliff walls, echoed back even louder.

The ground under Kelly's chair was shaking.

Then, suddenly, everything seemed to just . . . stop.

Silence.

Dead, heavy silence.

Kelly was afraid to even breathe.

Then the entire top of the machine, Magneto and all, appeared to vanish, leaving in its place a light that seemed to ooze rather than radiate, a light that filled everything around it, expanding outward.

Liquid light, creeping and unstoppable.

There was nothing like it in all of Kelly's experience.

And it was coming right at him.

He tried to shove back as the white light reached him, then washed up and over him, crawling into his eyes, his mouth, his ears, and flooding his mind.

He tried to scream, but the light muffled everything, filling his every pore, touching his every nerve with hot tips of agony combined with ecstasy. His senses ran through the range of everything he had ever experienced.

First every scent he had ever smelled, from baking

bread to an overused latrine. From a woman's perfume to the smell of fear when someone faced him in the Senate.

Then images started flashing through his mind, faster and faster, like a movie on fast forward. He was able to see everything he had ever done in his life. And then things others had done around him.

He saw it all.

Understood it all.

Then he heard over again what he had said. Everything, clear and distinct, all at once. And then what people had said around him. And about him.

He took it all in.

The touch of old girlfriends, of soft shirts, of burning plates.

He could feel every detail one moment, then nothing the next.

And then, far, far quicker than it had started, it was over.

The light just seemed to crawl back out of every pore, then vanish.

Inside the machine, Magneto slumped, clearly exhausted by what he had done. He looked drained. Mystique ran to him and supported him as he came down and slowly walked toward Kelly.

Kelly looked down at himself. His entire body seemed to be glowing under his clothes. His skin was glistening, almost luminescent.

"Oh, God," he said, crying now. "What have you done to me?"

He wanted to push back the memory of all the sensations, all the understanding, but they wouldn't be ignored. He knew the last few minutes could never be ignored.

Magneto stumbled over to a place in front of Kelly and weakly smiled. "Welcome to the future, brother."

Chapter Ten

X-Men Mansion

As Rogue slept soundly nearby, the dream returned to Logan. The nightmare.

The dream Logan knew was real. Had been real. But he could only remember the dream. And the nightmare.

And, of course, the pain.

Flash!

The military lab loomed over him, crazy instruments, older-looking stuff. Bottles, machines, tanks of fluid.

Bright lights filled the ceiling over him.

Belts held him down, secure to the bed.

The images were there, but never anything that could tell him where he was. What was outside the walls.

Flash!

He was naked. Someone in a mask had drawn on his body with blue pen, showing every branch of his skeleton. The person was a man, but Logan could see only the eyes. Cold eyes.

Others came in as Logan fought against the belts that held him. Rubber gloves.

Masks.

White gowns and hats.

104

Cold eyes.

One rubber-gloved hand shoved a mask over his mouth and nose. He struggled but lost the fight.

The air from the mask tasted metallic.

The images swam before him.

He could no longer fight. His body wouldn't respond to his thoughts.

They picked up the bed and lowered it, with him still strapped to it, into a tank of liquid

It sloshed around him.

Scalpels flashed over him.

A black figure loomed in his vision.

The scalpels cut.

Pain!

And cut.

Pain!

And cut.

Unbearable pain!

Flash!

He screamed.

Beside him a figure loomed out of the shadows.

He reacted. Instantly. Instinctively.

His hands weren't belted down as they had been in the dream. Yet he still thought he was in the nightmare.

Snikt. His claws cut through his attacker.

Silence.

His scream was long gone into the walls and hallways of the mansion around him.

He didn't move.

His attacker didn't move. Logan could feel the weight of whoever it was on his claws. And he heard the gasp of pain.

A familiar gasp.

His nightmare-fogged mind tried to wake up, remind himself where he was.

Suddenly his door burst open. Cyclops stood frozen there for an instant until Storm and Jean shoved past him, flipping on the light.

Logan was sitting upright in his bed. The claws from his right hand were still extended through Rogue's shoulder and out her back.

She was frozen on the end of his fist, standing beside his bed. He held her there, staring into her shocked eyes, not knowing if he should move or not.

What had he done?

Cyclops jumped to help, but Storm grabbed his arm. "Don't touch her."

Rogue nodded, then smiled at Logan. "You were having a nightmare," she said, her voice raspy.

"I know," Logan said.

Rogue eased one arm up slowly and gently touched his face, as if he were a long-lost lover and this would be the last time she would ever see him.

For a short moment her touch was light. Wonderful.

Then what felt like a blast of electric current shot through his body.

His claws instantly retracted, pulling through Rogue like a knife through butter.

Rogue staggered back, mouth open in a silent scream. Her eyes were wide with fear, with shock, with horror.

The electric charge stopped as suddenly as it had started, the moment her hand left the side of his face. Blackness threatened to swarm in from the sides of his mind and take him, but he shoved it back.

Rogue stood staring at him, with Cyclops, Storm, and Jean gathered around her but not touching her. And as they all watched, her wounds healed, leaving not even the slightest scar. She stood for a moment, a stunned look on her face. Then she bolted from the room.

His fuzzy mind wouldn't let him understand what had just happened. He was just glad that she was okay.

Then he couldn't hold the blackness back any longer. This time he didn't dream.

Twenty minutes later, Storm stood in the hall as Scott came out, leaving Jean and Professor Xavier to deal with Logan. She didn't need to be a telepath to see that Scott was angry. Deeply angry.

He nodded to her and stalked past.

"Scott, wait!" Storm said, moving to catch up with him.

He stopped, hands on his hips, daring her to say something. She had never seen him like this before. His visor was almost a bright red. Luckily he knew perfectly how to contain his power, especially during times like this. The alternative would be disastrous.

"You want to talk about it?" she asked, keeping her voice low so they wouldn't awake anyone in the rooms nearby.

"Not really," he said.

"Jealous of Logan, huh?" she asked, taking a chance.

Her words seemed to snap his head back as if she'd hit him.

"So," she said, pushing, "someone in your past had a problem with jealousy, huh?"

"None of your damn business," Scott said, keeping his voice low, but very cold and forceful. "And I'm not jealous. I just hate how Logan puts everything we've worked for at risk."

"So," Storm said, "what would you do? Throw him out on the street like—"

"Yes," Scott said, adjusting his visor. "I would. He's hurt Jean, and now Rogue."

"He didn't mean to," Storm countered.

"You tell yourself whatever you want," Cyclops said, "but the truth is this: We have a school here, filled with children. We're not ready to deal with this sort of—"

Now he had gotten her angry. And he wasn't going to get away with it. "Scott, this has nothing to do with the children, and you know it."

Cyclops shook his head, the strength in her words surprising him.

"Frankly," Storm said, pressing on and giving him no chance to say anything, "I am amazed that you would even put the children between yourself and the truth."

"You really think this is about Jean?" Cyclops said.

"Yes, I do," Storm said.

Cyclops took a deep breath and stared at her. His voice was still low and cold, and downright mean. "Jean can do whatever she wants. I am not in charge of her and have no desire to be in charge of her. How dare you even imply that I am."

At that, he turned and walked toward his and Jean's room.

"Scott, for God's sake . . ."

He stopped and looked back at her. "You saw what happened, Storm. Whatever else I may feel personally doesn't matter. Magneto is coming. And people are going to die."

With that, he stepped into his room. His door closed with a solid *thump*.

Storm forced herself to take a few deep breaths. That

hadn't been productive. She and Scott had had discussions in the past, and disagreements, but never an argument like this one.

She glanced back at Logan's door. Maybe Scott was right. Logan was hurting them in many, many ways. And this argument was just a small example.

What would be next? Who would be next?

Jean stood behind Professor Xavier, a good number of feet back from Logan's bed. The professor had said he was going to try to wake Logan up, to check if he was all right. He had told Scott to leave and had asked her to stay as backup. Clearly Scott hadn't liked that.

She would deal with one problem at a time.

"Ready?" the professor asked.

"When you are," she said.

You are perfectly safe now.

The professor was allowing her to hear what he was thinking.

Logan stirred and moaned, twisting on his bed like a child in the throes of a bad dream.

I want you to stay calm, and tell me if you understand what I'm saying.

Logan opened his eyes slowly and again moaned, reaching up and touching his head.

Do you understand me?

"Would you get the hell out of my head, cue ball!" Logan snarled.

Jean laughed, relieved. She could tell that the professor was also very pleased.

"Well," Professor Xavier said out loud, "I'd say you are recovering nicely."

The professor moved up closer to the bed, and Jean moved over and sat at the foot.

"How's Rogue? Is she okay? And what did she do to me?" Logan asked, holding his head. "I feel as if I've been on a ten-day bender."

"She borrowed your power," Jean said.

"Pardon me?" Logan responded, blinking at her. It was as if he was trying to focus his eyes.

"Rogue is like a conductor," the professor explained. "Any physical contact can cause unconsciousness, seizures, and even death to the one she touches."

"Not a fun mutation," Logan said. "And I've seen it at work before."

"It is not," the professor agreed. "With mutants, she's able to take on their gifts for a short time."

"In this case," Jean said, "your ability to heal."

"Well," Logan said, still holding his head with one hand, as if it might just fall apart if he let go. "It felt like she almost killed me."

"If she had held on any longer," the professor said, "she might have."

The professor glanced over at Jean, then back at Logan. "You should get some sleep now."

The professor turned and wheeled his chair out into the hallway. Jean stood and moved to stand beside Logan where he lay on the bed. "You need something, you shout."

Logan took her hand. His own hand was rough, hard, yet part of her didn't want him to let go.

"You know," he said, "I'd sleep better if you stayed with me."

She laughed and pulled away. "Somehow I doubt that, Logan."

"Yeah, so do I," Logan admitted.

"Good night, Logan," she said as she pulled his door closed.

She took a deep breath to settle her nerves, then headed for her room. Now all she had to do was get Scott calmed down and just maybe she could get some sleep. Maybe.

Chapter
Eleven

Magneto's Headquarters

Senator Kelly sat on the floor against the cold stone, wondering what to do, where to go, what was going to happen to him next.

He couldn't believe how much had changed in the last twelve hours. It almost seemed like a lifetime ago that he had climbed into the government helicopter, enjoying the fruits of his position. His public image had been rising in the polls, and the Mutant Registration Act was going to garner him a lot more free air time before it was finished.

Now this mutant—this Magneto—had done something to him. Something horrible that Kelly couldn't quite figure out yet. But he knew his body had changed. He could feel it. He seemed to be sweating all the time, even though he wasn't hot at all.

He stood and moved over to the cell's only window. The entire cell, including the window, had been cut out of the rock cliff face. Thick bars were implanted in the stone. The bars were just set close enough that when he leaned forward to stare at the ocean pounding on the rocks far below, he couldn't get his head through.

The door to the cell was set in the opposite wall, and it was also barred. The path to his cell wound around a far cliff wall, to a long walkway that was now retracted, leaving the cell without an exit.

He tried to think, make himself understand that he was being held hostage. He had to be thinking all the time; he had to stay on his toes, keep Magneto and his other mutant friends always wary of him. And he also had to find out what the machine had done to him.

He glanced down at his pants, and the shirt under his jacket. They were wet. His skin was wet. Yet he felt all right. Just tired. What was Magneto doing to him?

Why?

He tugged on one of the window's bars, then another, hoping that one of them might be loose. They weren't, and he knew he could never chip the base of one of them out of the stone—certainly not in time to help.

And even if he did somehow manage it, where would he go?

He pushed his face between two bars in frustration, desperately trying to look out and down, to see what lay below.

Suddenly it felt as if his skull cracked and got smaller. His head went a little farther between the bars.

He yanked back, shocked. He grabbed his head on both sides, feeling to see if something was wrong. If he had hurt himself.

What in the hell had just happened?

He could feel his head slowly expand back out in his hands, until it was a normal shape again.

"Okay," Kelly said aloud, his heart pounding, his breath coming in pants as he fought to keep himself under control. "There has to be a perfectly logical explanation."

He couldn't think of one.

He stepped back up to the bars and once again carefully leaned his head between two of them, letting the cold steel rub his forehead just outside his eyes.

Nothing.

Water dripped off his head. His hands. Everywhere. He leaned a little harder against the bars.

This time he could feel his head sort of scrunch up.

He pushed harder and harder, expecting it to hurt at any moment, until his head was halfway through the bars, with the steel rubbing both his ears. The process had made a loud crunching sound in his ears, and he could feel the motion, but it didn't seem painful at all.

He yanked back again, leaving wet marks on the bars.

Quickly his head returned to its normal size like a balloon filling with air.

He was losing his mind!

This couldn't be happening to him!

He kicked off his shoes and pulled off his soaked socks. Both shoes had standing water in them. Without the shoes he walked around the cell, trying to think, his bare feet leaving wet footprints on the rock floor.

Nothing made sense. Magneto had kidnapped him and had done something to him.

That much was clear.

But how could his head scrunch down enough to get between those bars, yet not hurt him?

Suddenly, across the gap outside the main door, Kelly heard footsteps on the stone. Someone was coming up the path to his cell.

He moved back over to the window. Then, out of pure desperation, he leaned forward and pressed his head between the bars.

It went more easily this time, and before he knew it, his head was through. Below he could see the water pounding the rocks. The fall would kill him, he was sure. But he had to get out of the cell, give himself some more time before Magneto took him.

Kelly turned his shoulder and, with both hands on the stone ledge, tried to pull his body through.

For an instant it wouldn't fit, then he heard the crunching as his shoulders and his rib cage collapsed, and he pulled himself through the small opening between the bars. He was halfway there.

Far, far below, the crashing waves shoved water into the air. There was a slight ledge just under the windowsill that seemed to go around the cliff for a short distance.

He pulled his hips through the small opening, feeling the bones smash down, then feeling them expand back to normal size as soon as the pressure was off.

This wasn't really happening to him.

From the pathway, he heard the extension ramp start across toward his cell door. He didn't have any more time. With speed born of desperation, he turned around on the rock windowsill and lowered himself down to the thin ledge. He'd never done anything like this before. His heart was pounding so hard he thought it was going to burst out of his chest.

He had read where people in stressful situations often did things they would never dream of doing under normal conditions. Well, this certainly qualified.

As the ramp stopped, the sound rang through the cell

so loudly it made Kelly freeze. Then, as the lock clicked, Kelly tried to move to his right along the thin rock ledge, grasping for any handhold to get himself away from the window. But with his fingers and hands so wet, it felt as if he were holding on to a wall of ice.

"How are we feeling, Senator?" Magneto asked as the cell door swung open with a clank. "Advanced, I hope? Senator?"

There was a very long pause. Kelly tried to hold his breath, hoping they wouldn't look out here.

Suddenly, over his head, the steel bars of the window were ripped inward, pulled out of the stone as if it were putty.

A moment later Magneto stuck his head out and smiled. "Senator, did you actually squeeze through these bars? That is very impressive."

Kelly was barely holding on. His hands were wet, his feet slick on the stone. "What have you done to me?" he croaked.

"Senator," Magneto said, "this is pointless. Where would you go? Who would take you in now that you are one of us?"

Kelly couldn't believe what he had just heard. Magneto had referred to him as one of them.

A mutant!

Then, in a flash, he understood.

"You changed me into a mutant?" Kelly asked in horror.

Magneto smiled. "Of course. What did you think I was doing to you?"

Then Magneto moved back out of the window and Kelly heard him say, as if in a faraway dream, "Sabretooth, get the senator off that ledge."

A moment later an ugly face thrust out the window, and a clawlike hand reached for him.

Kelly, at that moment, no longer cared. He had become his worst nightmare. He had become the very thing that he hated most.

He pushed back away from the stone even as Sabretooth grabbed his hand and coat.

But Kelly felt his hand crunch down into something so small and slick that Sabretooth couldn't hold on.

And then, looking back into the face of the monster with yellow hair, Kelly fell toward the water below.

It was a very, very long fall.

Chapter
Twelve

X-Men Mansion

This time the nightmare didn't carry Logan all the way down into the pain and the cutting. He came awake, almost wide awake, staring at the ceiling. He had been sweating, and the sheets were soaking wet. It took him a moment to remember exactly where he was.

Then he remembered.

Remembered what had happened last night with Rogue.

Remembered the feeling of death.

A noise snapped his head toward the door. A strange-looking kid was peeking inside. His eyes grew wide when he saw Logan turn. The kid made a little squeaking noise that sounded like "Sorry," and then ducked out, pulling the door shut behind him.

Logan laughed. Then he rubbed his face and head, hard, trying to shake the sensations, the memory of what had happened with Rogue. And what he had felt when she touched him.

Then he realized he didn't want to lose that memory. In fact, it just might be one of the more important things that had ever happened to him.

For the next thirty minutes he lay there, thinking. Remembering.

Even though she wasn't hungry, Rogue had a small tray of food: a sandwich, a banana, and some milk. The day had turned beautiful, almost springlike in its warmth. Four of the other kids, including Kitty, were sitting on a stone wall above the garden, eating and talking. She knew, after how all the kids had treated her this morning, that she didn't dare try to go sit with them.

Or with anyone else for that matter. She was back to being alone. As alone as she had been hitchhiking. And for the same reason. Her curse.

Her problem.

Or as they called it here, her power.

She walked past the group on the wall, looking for a place to sit in the garden. But no space was open. Behind her she could hear a few of the kids whispering loudly. She knew they were whispering about her.

She moved out of the garden and toward the basketball court. Some of the older kids were playing a pickup game. Jubilee stood to one side with four others. She looked up and saw Rogue, then turned away, making it very clear that Rogue couldn't join them.

Yesterday they had all been so friendly. Today they hated her. Feared her. Just as her friends and family at home had feared her.

Rogue moved away from the game, down a path leading into the woods. There she found a small stone bench and sat, putting the tray beside her. She could feel the tears trying to come up, but she wouldn't let them.

"Get a grip!" she said firmly to herself. She had been alone before; she could be alone again. She knew she wasn't going to be cured. She had better get used to this, and do it now.

"Rogue?"

She spun around to see Bobby moving up the path through the trees toward her. She turned back to her food, pretending to be interested in it.

"Rogue," Bobby said, "what did you do?"

He had stopped and was actually talking to her. The first one all day.

"I didn't mean to touch him," Rogue said. Her resolve slipped, and the tears started to come. "I didn't know what to do."

"They're saying you steal other mutants' powers," Bobby said, standing a few feet away, as if she had some terrible disease.

"That's not true," Rogue said. "I mean, not really—"

"You don't ever use your power against another mutant," Bobby said forcefully. Accusingly.

"But I had no choice," she said weakly. She knew she had had a choice. She could have died. And at the moment, she knew that that would have been the better choice.

"If I were you," Bobby said, stepping away even farther, "I'd get myself out of here."

She looked up at the fear in his eyes. "What do you mean?"

"I mean the students are all freaked," he said. "So am I. And Professor Xavier is furious. I don't know what he'll do with you. I just think it would be easier for you on your own."

Rogue just couldn't stop the tears now. She sat there sobbing as Bobby slowly backed away.

"Rogue," Bobby said before he turned. "You really should go."

He turned his back on her and walked toward the sounds of the basketball game. The kids there were laughing and shouting and having fun.

She knew that that wasn't going to be something she would ever be allowed to do again. Just as she had done at home, she had to leave. For her own best interests, and for everyone around her.

She forced herself to stop crying. She couldn't afford to cry anymore.

She picked up the banana and put it in her pocket. Then she took a large bite out of the sandwich, even though she still wasn't hungry. No telling when she would get anything to eat again.

Then she stood, and without a look back, headed down the path into the woods, drinking the milk as she walked.

Behind her the sounds of the laughter slowly faded. And with it, all her hope for a better life.

Somewhere along the Atlantic Coast

Twenty-seven-year-old Bonnie Risk had decided it was just too nice a day to stay indoors. She and her seven-year-old son Neal needed to get out, especially since it was Saturday and Neal's father had gone in to work. They lived a short fifteen minutes away from their favorite beach, and Bonnie had figured there wouldn't be many people there this time of the year, even on a weekend.

She had been right. Maybe only a dozen others strolled the beach or sat watching the waves. The sun was just warm enough for her to spread a towel and sit comfortably while Neal played nearby. This was better than the summer, since there weren't many people and it wasn't hot and humid.

"Mom!" Neal shouted. "Look!"

Something was coming up out of the water. A very strange something. First there was a head, then shoulders, then arms—with flippers.

Bonnie quickly scrambled over to Neal and stood, grasping his shoulders so he wouldn't move.

The thing looked half fish, half human. It also had flipperlike feet, and a human face. A very familiar human face, actually.

She watched as the creature came up out of the water. By the time it reached dry sand, its flippers had turned back into feet and arms.

It was a man. A very naked man now, who walked forward, clearly disgusted, clearly angry, dripping water. He veered toward where she had been sitting, grabbed her towel off the sand, and wrapped it around himself. She almost shouted for him to stop, but at that instant he turned and looked at her and she realized who it was.

Senator Robert Kelly!

Just a few days before, she had spent most of a day watching his Senate hearings on television. Senate hearings investigating mutants. But if he was a mutant himself, why did he hate the other mutants so much? More than ever, nothing in politics made sense to her.

He glared at her as she clutched Neal close to her side.

"Mom?" Neal said, loud enough for Kelly to hear. "Is that a mutant?"

Kelly sneered contemptuously, then turned and started toward the street and parking lot. Halfway there, he suddenly bent over, clutching his stomach as if in extreme pain. Then she heard him moan as he dropped to one knee, his head down.

"Stay here!" she ordered Neal.

She started toward Kelly to see what she could do to help him. Mutant or not, senator or not, he was still human, and it looked like he needed help. But before she could take two steps, he had straightened up, stood, and started walking again.

She stopped, dumbfounded, as he moved away. Then, with a shrug, she moved back to Neal, murmuring under her breath. "Hypocritical politicians."

There was no doubt about it—this was one trip to the beach they were both going to remember for a very long time.

Chapter Thirteen

X-Men Mansion

Professor Xavier held up the X rays and studied them again, looking for anything that might give him a clue as to why Magneto was after Logan. Clearly there must be a reason, and that reason was somehow important to what Magneto was planning.

The door to the medical lab clicked and opened as the professor put down one X ray and held up another. Without turning, he knew it was Scott who had just come in. He could sense the anger in his young team leader.

"What are you looking for, Scott?" he asked, still without turning around.

The young X-Man slipped up on top of a lab bed and shook his head. "Nothing, really. Any luck finding Magneto with the Cerebro?"

"No. And it's strange," Xavier said. The fact that he couldn't find Magneto bothered Xavier a lot. Somehow Magneto was shielding himself against the Cerebro, which might mean that others in the brotherhood could do so as well, if Magneto wanted them to.

Xavier put down another X ray and picked up a third, continuing to study.

"There are far more powerful mutants than Logan," Scott said. "Why is this one so important to him?"

Xavier turned and glanced at Scott. It was clear, even without reading the young man's mind, that he was very troubled. "You don't like him, do you?"

Scott almost snorted. "How can you tell?" he asked sarcastically.

Xavier smiled. "Well, I'm psychic, you know."

Scott laughed.

"Logan could be a valuable addition here," Xavier said, staring at the young leader.

"He's not one of us," Scott replied.

"But he is," Xavier said, as forcefully as he dared. "Don't ever forget that."

"Fine," Scott said. "But you put a guy like that in a combat situation, there's no way he's going to take orders."

Xavier stared at Scott. "Give him an order worth following, and he'll take it."

Scott nodded, adjusted his glasses, still not happy. "He's not a team player."

Xavier laughed softly. "Neither were you, Scott, when you first arrived. Remember?"

Scott was about to respond when the door slammed open. Logan stood there, clearly upset. Professor Xavier could tell exactly what he was thinking, and it wasn't good.

"She's gone!" Logan said.

"Who?" Scott asked, dropping down off the table.

"Rogue," Xavier said.

Logan nodded.

The professor stretched out his mind until he found who he was looking for. *Storm. Jean. Meet us at Cerebro. Rogue has disappeared.*

"Come with me," Xavier said out loud to Cyclops and Logan, moving his chair past Cyclops and toward the door. Logan quickly stepped aside.

Xavier turned his chair to the right and headed for the thick steel door at the end of the hallway. Beyond it was a room in which he had spent much time over the past week, looking for Magneto without success.

From the elevator, Storm and Jean burst into the hall.

"What are we doing?" Logan demanded, staring at the others as they all approached Cerebro's polished steel door. "Why aren't we looking for her?"

"We are," Cyclops said.

Xavier moved his chair up to a panel positioned at his eye level beside the door. The screen lit up, registering his presence, and he let it scan his eyes and forehead. A measure to keep out those who shouldn't have access to Cerebro, including any of the school's inquisitive students.

A moment later the security computer recognized him and the massive steel door clicked loudly, then started to open.

"The brain waves of mutants are different than average human beings," Xavier said, explaining to Logan as they moved along. "Cerebro is a device which amplifies my power, allowing me to locate mutants over great distances."

"That's how you followed the Sabretooth guy," Logan said, nodding. "And found me and Rogue."

"It is."

"Welcome, Professor," the computer voice said as they all moved inside.

Xavier nodded as he caught a wave of amazement from Logan, who was impressed at the size of the room in which they stood. It was big, completely round, and had only one entrance and exit. It was, the professor explained, simply described, a radio antenna for brain waves.

The entrance had led them to a small platform at the center of one wall. The platform was engineered to extend out so that the operator was dropped directly in the center of the sphere.

"Well," Logan said, looking around, "this certainly is a big, round room. Why don't you just use this to find Magneto?"

"I've been trying," Xavier said as he moved into position. "But he seems to have found a way to shield himself from it."

Logan stared at him. "Just how would he know how to do that?"

"Because he helped me build it."

Logan's face registered shock that would have been almost amusing at any other time. But right now they had to find Rogue. And fast, before something happened to her.

"Would you excuse me?" Xavier said to the rest.

Jean quickly set a few controls on the main board; then all of them moved back to the hallway. Slowly the door closed, blocking them out—and blocking out all other thoughts from the mutants in the building.

Xavier tapped a button on his chair, and a headset lowered quickly from the ceiling. As it did, the room seemed to come to life. The walls seemed to move away, slowly at first, then faster and faster, until their movement was no longer visible.

The ramp and headset slowly extended into the center of the large room, coming to a stop at the exact point where his head was located—the exact center of Cerebro.

Suddenly, all around him, the wall seemed to move outward, away from him.

Exploding.

Until he was simply alone, sitting in a black void.

Then he let his mind climb, up out of the basement, out of the mansion. The light above seemed bright, but he knew he wasn't seeing it with his eyes. Just with his brain.

Soon he could feel Rogue.

Jean had set the Cerebro to focus on Rogue's brain waves, and it was taking him to her.

He felt like a bird, free of the wheelchair and of his body, flashing over the trees, the roads, the houses. He let himself go. Everything seemed like a blur of color, yet he knew he could stop at any moment, to seek out any detail. The surroundings were more like a movie in fast forward.

He could sense Rogue's brain waves, the power of her personality, pulling him toward her.

Down he went—over a building, over other people— until he finally saw her, sitting on a bench alone. He eased into her mind, without letting her know he was there, until he saw what she saw. He felt her fear, her sadness, and what had made her run away.

He would take care of the other students after he

knew exactly where she was. Once she was safe and sound.

As he carefully searched her mind for her location, she helped him without knowing it. She looked up at an Arrivals/Departures board, and he knew exactly where she was.

A moment later he was back in Cerebro, the ramp withdrawing, the door swinging open.

Logan stared for a moment at the closed door, then at Jean. For the last minute or so no one had said a word. He had simply paced. Storm and Cyclops had sat on the floor. Jean had stood near Cerebro's control panel, watching it intently.

"What's it like?" Logan asked, finally unable to stand the silence anymore. "This Cerebro thing he's using."

"I've never used Cerebro," Jean said. "It takes a certain degree of control."

"And I'm not prepared to see your memory erased," Cyclops said.

Logan looked at her sharply, and she nodded. Then she glanced at the panel. "He's coming out."

They all gathered around as the massive steel door opened, like an ultramodern bank vault. Professor Xavier wheeled out and looked up at Cyclops. "She's a few miles up the road. At the train station."

"I'll go," Logan said, starting to turn away.

"You can't leave the mansion, Logan," Xavier said. "It's just the opportunity that Magneto needs."

Logan turned and faced the professor straight on. "Yeah, but I'm the reason she took off."

The hard eyes of the professor looked back at him

without blinking. "We had a deal, Logan. Forty-eight hours."

Logan nodded. He had made that deal. But he felt responsible for Rogue.

"She's all right, Logan," Jean said. "She's just upset."

"Storm, Cyclops," Xavier said, turning toward them. "Go see if you can talk to her."

Cyclops nodded, and they both headed off at a run to the ready room, to change into the black uniforms.

"Jean, we have to talk to the rest of the students," the professor said.

Jean nodded, and the two of them moved to the elevator, leaving Logan standing there, fuming.

A deal was a deal. He knew that.

He started to follow the professor and Jean, then stopped. This was Rogue. And she could be in danger. He wouldn't allow that to happen. Besides, while Cyclops and Storm changed clothes, Rogue might get away. Or worse.

To hell with the deal. Sometimes responsibility had to take precedence.

To hell with this Magneto character, too. What had happened last night to Rogue was more important to him.

He turned and moved quickly down the hallway to the door that led into the mansion's underground garage. Unlike the hangar, with its one special plane, this garage was filled with all sorts of vehicles, all painted black.

A black motorcycle sat to one side, a black helmet sitting on the seat. He knocked the helmet aside and climbed on, kicking the bike into life. He could feel the power of the machine, clearly souped up and well tuned. Nothing like a powerful bike to give a guy a sense of confidence.

He popped it into gear; then, with the back tire spinning, he headed out into the deepening night.

Behind him he heard faint shouting. And ignored it.

Chapter Fourteen

Westchester Train Station

Rogue moved down the aisle of the train until she found two empty seats. She hoped the car wasn't going to be crowded. She didn't want anyone sitting next to her. Across the aisle, a young woman and child were playing together, laughing lightly. She couldn't imagine ever being that happy again.

Outside the window, people stood on the old wooden platform, talking, saying good-bye to friends, or just waiting. They all looked normal. More than likely they all led normal lives. She wondered how she looked to them.

"Hey, kid," a voice said.

She glanced up as Logan dropped into the spot beside her, smiling.

She turned back to face the window without saying a word. There was nothing she could say to him. She had almost killed him last night. She had no idea what he was even doing here.

"You runnin' again?" Logan asked.

"How did you know I was here?" Rogue asked without turning her face away from the window.

"Well," Logan said, "the professor put on this metal head thing, and—" He waved his hand in disgust. "Don't ask."

"Sorry I did," she said.

"You even have a ticket?"

"No," Rogue said. She had figured she would deal with that problem once the train started moving. Even if they kicked her off, she would still be farther from the mansion than she had been.

"Then let me give you some free advice," Logan said. "When the ticket guy comes, hide in the bathroom. You won't have to pay that way."

She nodded. She had no idea why he was helping her. Or if he was even going to ride along with her. Finally she just had to know what he knew. She turned from the window to face him. "I hear the professor was mad at me."

Logan half snorted. "Why would he be mad at you?"

"Because I used my power on another mutant," Rogue said. "And I'm never supposed to."

Logan looked at her, clearly puzzled. "Who told you that?"

"Bobby," Rogue said softly.

"One of the other students?" Logan asked.

"Yes," Rogue said.

"And you didn't go ask the professor or Storm or Jean? Or even Scott?"

Rogue shook her head. It just hadn't occurred to

her. Bobby seemed as if he knew what he was talking about.

Logan sighed and said nothing.

X-Men Mansion

Bobby stood in front of the heavy steel door that led to Cerebro, just staring at it as if it might open of its own accord. Of course, it wouldn't. He glanced around, making sure no one was coming in either direction. Then he started to shift.

Quickly Mystique moved back into the shape of her own body. She took a moment to draw a breath, then focused on what she needed to do next. She had to remember the exact patterns, the exact details. Everything needed to be perfect. Especially the eyes. Being young Bobby had been easy. She had fooled the girl Rogue, just as they had planned. But this shift had to be exact. And that was something she hadn't done often.

With her most intense focus, she started to shift again. This time just changing part of herself.

She focused on every detail in her mind, as she shifted from the shoulders up into a replica of Professor Xavier.

When she was finished, she keyed in a sequence that opened the panel near the door, then knelt down slightly in front of the retinal scanner. It lit up, scanning her forehead and eyes.

For a moment she thought it might not work.

Then, with a satisfying clanking sound, the door unlocked and slowly swung open.

She quickly shifted back to her natural form and stepped inside. She turned and pulled the door almost closed behind her, making sure it didn't latch. She hoped anyone passing by would not notice the slightly open door, but she also didn't want to be trapped inside this machine. That was for sure.

"Welcome, Professor," the machine said.

She didn't answer. Magneto had told her to be very careful about that. He had no idea what safety features Charles Xavier had added lately.

Mystique quickly moved to the console near the edge of the platform. The massive round room remained completely dark around her, but she had practiced hundreds of times what she was going to do next. She didn't need light.

She swung in under the console and with a small screwdriver opened the panel she found there.

A bright white light covered her. It came from a beautiful, intricate, fiber-optic core that was suspended under the panel. It seemed almost like a ball of energy.

Or a brain. More like a glowing white brain.

She studied it for a moment, then quickly jammed the screwdriver into it, again and again.

After a couple dozen hits, the light faded, leaving only gray tubes, broken wires, and dripping fluid.

She had killed it.

Ten minutes later, again in the shape of the student named Bobby, she headed out one of the mansion's side doors and into the garden.

The real Bobby sat in his room, studying, wondering

why Rogue had left. Feeling vaguely guilty for not defending her, and hoping she was all right.

Westchester Train Station

Cyclops glanced over at Storm as he brought the black SUV to a halt in front of the train station. The black motorcycle Logan had taken was parked there.

"Let's hope he's talking some sense into her," Storm said.

"I'm more concerned about keeping Logan out of Magneto's hands."

"Yes, that too," Storm agreed.

They headed inside the classic station house. It boasted high, beamed ceilings; massive decorative windows; and a clock tower that could be seen from the tracks and parklike grounds. At least a hundred people were milling about, sitting on the high-backed wooden benches or standing in groups, talking. Cyclops could see a train sitting on the tracks just beyond the building.

"Split up," Cyclops said. "You check the ticket counter. I'll see if I can spot her in the benches, or on the platform outside."

Storm nodded as Cyclops turned and headed into the crowd of people.

Logan leaned back in the train seat and let out a deep breath. Things had changed so fast for him, and for Rogue, it was no wonder she had believed the other student. She had nothing else to believe, no one to trust. Neither did he, really. But there was something about this professor and his people that Logan liked.

Now he had to get Rogue back there, for her own good.

"You know," Logan said, staring up at the ceiling as he talked, "I woke up one day in the woods, in the middle of nowhere. I had no memories, no life."

He turned and looked straight at her. She was watching him, listening. He held up his fist, showing her the marks on his hands where his claws were, just below the skin. "I didn't know where these had come from. All I had was the dreams of pain that wouldn't let me sleep."

She nodded, so he went on.

"At first I couldn't live with it. I can't even show you all the scars from all the times I tried to kill myself, cause they just disappeared. I looked at this power of mine as a curse."

Again she nodded, agreeing with him there.

"When you touched me last night," he said, going slow and not looking at her, "I felt, for one brief second, death. And right then I realizcd I didn't like it. I realized I didn't want it anymore."

A tear was slowly making its way down Rogue's cheek.

"I just came to thank you for that."

She nodded, saying nothing.

And there was nothing more he could say.

Around them a few other people came onto the car and took seats, getting ready for the trip. Logan had no idea where this train was even headed. He doubted Rogue did, either.

"You think I should go back?" Rogue asked softly.

"I think you should follow your instincts," Logan said.

Slowly, sitting there, arms folded around herself, she began to cry. Soft sobs shook her small frame without making any noise.

He took his jacket off and carefully wrapped it around her shoulders. She tried to pull away from his touch, even through the leather, but he held her firmly. Finally she gave in and sobbed into his shoulder as he held her.

After a moment the sobs slowed.

"There are not many people who will understand what you're going through, Rogue," Logan said with uncharacteristic softness. "But I think this guy Xavier is one of them. And he seems to genuinely want to help you. That's a rare thing for people like us."

The train whistle echoed down the platform, and the train slowly jerked into motion. "What do you say?" Logan asked. "We can still get off at the next station, hop a cab, give these geeks one more shot."

Rogue was clearly thinking about it, but not yet convinced.

"Come on," Logan said. "I'll take care of you."

The words were out of his mouth before he'd even realized he said them.

Rogue looked up at him, her big eyes full of hope. "You promise?"

Logan took a deep breath. He actually did feel like taking care of this girl. He wasn't sure why. Partially, he felt as if he owed her. But mostly it just felt right to care about someone else besides himself for a change.

"Yeah, I promise," he said.

Then he frowned at her.

"What?"

"No more heart-to-hearts, though, okay?" Logan said. "I can't tell you how much I hate this."

Rogue laughed, smiling. "Deal."

Around them, people were talking and the car was rattling as the train slowly began to gain speed.

Suddenly everything lurched violently, and the train came to an almost instant stop, as if it had hit something very, very large.

Logan tried to catch himself, but it happened too fast. He went flying head over heels into the aisle, ending up flat on his back with a man in a business suit sprawled across his legs.

What the hell had they hit?

People were screaming and moaning and trying frantically to get to their feet.

He got out from under the guy and stood up. At a glance he could see that Rogue was all right. She looked as if she'd bumped her head, but she was moving fine.

The car around them creaked and rocked again, sending more shouts and screams echoing through the air.

Then the train started backward down the tracks.

Chapter Fifteen

Westchester Train Station

Storm moved through the crowd, ignoring the looks her black X-Men uniform elicited from the people. She was proud to be wearing it, and she hoped that someday everyone would recognize it as a sign of their goodwill and noble intentions.

For the moment, though, she moved up past three people who were standing in line at the ticket counter. "Excuse me," she said to them. "Emergency."

Then she turned to the ticket agent. "I was wondering if you could help me? I'm looking for a young girl, about seventeen. She's my height and has brown hair. She may have been upset."

The guy in the cage hadn't looked up at her until she was finished. "Nope, haven't noticed anyone like that—"

Suddenly the guy's eyes went wide with fear, and he quickly stepped back.

It took Storm an instant to realize that he was looking over her shoulder, not at her. She spun around just in time to come face-to-face with Sabretooth.

He was wearing a long trench coat to cover his furs,

but he still smelled like he'd come right out of a grave-yard. Before she could even move, he knocked a young boy aside, then grabbed her around the neck and lifted her off the ground, choking her.

She couldn't yell.

She couldn't even breathe.

Around them people backed away.

"Scream for me," Sabretooth said. Then he laughed. It was a vicious laugh.

Suddenly she could feel the professor inside her head. *Hold on, Storm. Fight! I'm with you.*

She kicked at Sabretooth, smashing her foot right into his midsection.

One woman screamed, and people started to run as he took Storm and smashed her backward into the glass of the ticket counter. The impact knocked some of the wind out of her, and shattered the glass, but it also loosened Sabretooth's grip on her neck.

She took a quick breath before he tightened his grip again.

This time he held her far enough away that she couldn't kick him.

Behind him she saw Cyclops fighting his way through scrambling people. Then she saw Toad jump up on a pillar behind him.

Try as she might, she couldn't shout out a warning.

Toad's tongue whipped out and snatched away Cyclops' visor, yanking his head up and back.

A massive red beam of energy shot out of Cyclops' eyes, before he could get them closed. Luckily it streaked upward. The beam ripped a hole in the roof of the building.

"Everyone get back!" he shouted, his voice carrying with authority over all the shouting and yelling. "Storm!"

Bits of stone and concrete and wood rained down on the crowd, sending people screaming and turning the panic up to a higher pitch. Now people were fighting and climbing over one another to get out of the building.

Sabretooth just laughed and choked her harder. If he held her like this too much longer he would break her neck.

Cyclops dropped to the floor, his eyes tight, completely blind. She was, for the moment, going to have to fight alone.

She reached out for the feeling of the weather around her. A moment later she could feel it bending to her control.

Lightning.

She needed lightning.

She could feel the professor in her mind, helping her, boosting her power.

Suddenly the lightning was there, and it was in her control.

She smashed the bolt down between them, bringing it in as close as she could to Sabretooth without touching either him or her.

The impact of the lightning and the resulting explosion ripped her from his grip and smashed her backward over the ticket counter. She rolled as she had trained to do, time and again in the danger room, and came up hard against a wall.

Sabretooth flew through the air in the other direction,

smashing through the Arrivals/Departures board, shattering it, sending clouds of dust and debris raining down over the remainder of the crowds.

Storm managed to pull herself to her feet, trying to catch her breath, just in time to watch Toad pick up the stunned Sabretooth and stagger away toward the train platform.

Cyclops was still on the ground, his eyes closed tight, his face pointed downward to make sure he would injure no one should any stray energy slip free.

She had no idea what had happened to Logan or Rogue. And the professor was no longer in her mind to tell her.

The lights had gone out inside the train, and the sound of metal buckling and folding surrounded Rogue. It was so loud it hurt her ears. It was as if a giant was tearing apart the train car.

People were screaming and trying to shove their way through the doors. She had braced herself between seats, and Logan had done the same in front of her. The smell of burning wires and smoke was starting to choke the car, as well.

She couldn't imagine how the train was moving backward. The ground was flat. Clearly something had to be pulling or pushing them.

Suddenly, with a massive tearing sound, the entire back of the car seemed to rip away. Everyone in the car except Rogue and Logan scrambled to get out the front door.

As Rogue watched, the figure of a man floated up and stood in the ripped-out area of the car. Rogue knew instantly it must be Magneto. If the professor was right, he was here to take Logan.

Magneto floated toward them, the car's metal walls and ceiling rippling like water as he moved.

Logan stepped into the aisle, his claws out.

"You must be Wolverine," Magneto said. "I saw your tags."

Before Logan could even say a word, Magneto held up a fist, and Logan just froze.

Magneto smiled, looking Logan over. "The remarkable metal doesn't run through your entire body, does it?"

Magneto opened his hand.

Logan's arms and legs spread out like a starfish. The pain was excruciating.

"I guess it does after all," Magneto said, laughing.

"Cute trick," Logan said.

Suddenly Logan started to sweat as Magneto pulled his claws out, more and more.

"Stop it!" Rogue shouted, and started toward Magneto. "Stop it now!"

"What the hell do you want with me?" Logan demanded.

"My dear boy," Magneto said, laughing still, "Whoever said I wanted you?"

Magneto glanced over at Rogue. His eyes were cold and dark.

She couldn't believe it. He was after her! Why? What did she have? What had she done to him?

"No!" Logan shouted, struggling futilely against the force that held him in its grip.

Magneto just shook his head and closed his fist.

Logan flew backward, smashing into the front wall of the train car. He slumped to the ground, unconscious.

"What did you do?" Rogue shouted, jumping out into the aisle and running toward Logan.

Suddenly she felt a sharp stabbing in the back of her neck. Before she could even reach up and touch the syringe that had jabbed her, the blackness swept over her.

She staggered two more steps and fell short of Logan, facedown on the train floor.

The last thing she remembered was hearing Magneto laughing, as if from a long, long distance away.

Chapter Sixteen

Westchester County, NY

Jean Grey faded the black Bentley Turbo into the corner, half watching the road, half watching Professor Xavier. The tires screamed and held as she accelerated out of the corner, pushing the car as fast as it and the roads would allow.

The professor was belted securely into the passenger seat, and his attention clearly wasn't on her or her driving. She knew it was at the train station, with Cyclops and Storm and Rogue and Logan. She could sense enough to know that the four of them were locked in the fight of their lives.

She took the next corner just a little too fast, and the rear end swung around, but she recovered without losing any speed. They were still a good ten miles away.

At this speed that would take them ten minutes.

Ten minutes too long.

Westchester Train Station

Magneto watched as Sabretooth and Toad quickly loaded the unconscious Rogue into the cloth bag and pulled the top closed. That would keep her from touching anyone if she woke up a little sooner than he had planned.

Logan was still out cold.

"What shall I do with this piece of garbage?" Sabretooth asked, kicking him.

"Leave him," Magneto said. "Bring the girl."

Sabretooth growled, kicked Logan once more, then turned to follow.

They moved as a group across the platform, through the edge of the train station, and out one of the doors that led to the front area. He half expected to see Charles' two flunkies appear and try again to stop them. Instead what greeted them were at least ten police cars, fanned out in front of them. Their flashers were lighting the shadowy trees and train station with strobes of blue and red.

At least twenty police officers had their guns drawn and were facing Magneto. Onlookers and the people who had been in the station had been shoved back a good hundred yards, clearing the parklike area in front of the station. *Good,* Magneto thought, because that was where he had planned to have Mystique land the helicopter.

"Seems they wanted to say good-bye to us," he said wryly.

One cop raised a megaphone. "Put your hands over your heads."

Magneto, Toad, and Sabretooth kept walking, with Rogue secure in the bag slung over Sabretooth's shoulder. Toad still carried Cyclops' visor, as if it were a trophy. Magneto hadn't expected this resistance, but it didn't really matter.

"I said raise your hands, jerk!" the cop ordered again.

Magneto shook his head. It seemed it was time again to teach the poor humans a lesson in manners. And also show them just how powerful mutantkind could be.

So he did raise his hands, but with them came two of the police cars. The two vehicles flew into the air and smashed back to earth with an impact that shook the ground.

The cops scattered, all guns still drawn and pointed at Magneto. With his mind Magneto felt the guns, and with a smooth downward snap of his hand he yanked all the guns out of every cop's hand. They flew toward him, and stopped.

He then turned the weapons around, still hovering in midair, and held them there, each aimed at a cop's face. A couple of the cops tried to dodge, but each gun remained with its owner. Pointed right between the eyes.

"You *Homo sapiens* and your guns," Magneto said, loudly enough for everyone to hear. "When will you ever learn?"

He was about to start the lesson when a hand grabbed his shoulder and spun him around. With his mind he maintained control over the floating firearms.

It was Sabretooth.

The savage mutant grabbed him by the throat and lifted him into the air. From his new vantage point, Magneto could see Toad moving to help his clawed companion. The grip hurt and he was having trouble breathing, but he knew it wasn't as tight as it could be.

"That's enough, Eric," Sabretooth said, almost as a growl.

"Let the cops go!" Toad demanded.

Magneto knew instantly who his real enemy was. He glanced around, trying to spot Charles, but without any luck.

"Why not come out where I can see you, Charles?" he said hoarsely.

Sabretooth gripped his throat even tighter, cutting off his wind for a moment, then relaxing just enough so that he could talk.

"What do you want her for?" Sabretooth asked, his voice an even lower growl, as if he was trying to fight Xavier's control.

Magneto reached up and tapped the side of his helmet. "What's the matter, Charles? Can't read my mind? So what now?"

"The girl?" Xavier asked through Sabretooth. "What do you want her for?"

"To save the girl," Magneto said, "you'll have to kill me. And what will that accomplish, Charles? You'll let these humans have their way, and they'll have you in chains with a number burned into your forehead."

"It's not going to be that way," Xavier responded through his unwilling proxy.

"Then kill me and find out," Magneto challenged. He knew Charles wouldn't do that. It wasn't who Charles was.

The seconds ticked past. Sabretooth's hand didn't move.

As Magneto had gambled, Charles would not kill an old friend.

"Release me," Magneto demanded.

Still, Sabretooth's hand didn't lighten its grip. It was starting to bite into Magneto's throat and skin. And his breathing was coming harder and harder.

"No?" Magneto said. "Then fine."

The gunshot echoed over the silent park in front of the old train station.

A number of screams sounded in the crowd down the block.

Without letting go of Magneto's throat, Sabretooth, under Xavier's directions, turned to see where the shot had come from.

Magneto laughed throatily. He had fired at point-blank range into the face of one cop, then had stopped the bullet just as it touched the man's skin. The bullet was still hanging there, the heat from it burning the man's forehead. The cop's eyes were huge, and Magneto had no doubt the poor fool had wet his pants from the fear.

The sound of the shot echoed off into the distance, and again the area was deadly quiet.

Charles, through Sabretooth, still hadn't let go of Magneto's neck.

"You want more?" Magneto asked.

Every gun floating in front of every cop cocked.

Two or three of the policemen dropped to their knees. The guns followed.

Two others dove and rolled, trying to get away. The guns followed, pointing in their faces when they stopped.

"Care to press your luck, Charles?" Magneto asked. "I can fire them all at once, but I don't think I can stop all the bullets."

The man with the bullet pressed against his forehead looked as if he was about to faint.

Sabretooth let go of Magneto and staggered back.

Toad looked around, half stunned.

"Still unwilling to make sacrifices, eh, Charles," Magneto said. "That's what makes you weak."

Sabretooth stiffened. "No, Eric," Sabretooth said, directed once again by Xavier. "That's what makes me strong."

Then Sabretooth slumped as the professor let him go again.

"Feeling a little used?" Magneto asked Sabretooth.

Sabretooth only growled.

Magneto looked around him at all the cops. Their guns were cocked, ready to fire.

Over the trees on the other side of the train station his helicopter flashed into sight. Mystique took it in a wide arc, then set it down expertly in the open area beside where they stood.

Magneto kept all the guns pointed at the cops as Toad loaded the sack containing their prize into the helicopter. Then he and Sabretooth climbed in.

Magneto waved to the cops, smiling. Then he climbed in and took the copilot's seat, still maintaining his hold on the guns. "Good-bye, Charles," he said.

He had no doubt that Charles could hear him.

Then, as they lifted off, he waved again, letting the guns drop to the ground.

Half the cops slumped. Two started throwing up.

All Magneto could do was laugh.

Jean pulled the Bentley onto a short side road and turned off the engine. The professor knew that his three people were just coming out of the trees. He had directed them away from the station and the authorities. They weren't in any shape to deal with the police, and the police weren't in any mood to deal with any more mutants at this point. Better to just let them think that Magneto and his people were the ones who did the damage.

"You better help them," he said to Jean as three figures stepped out from among the trees.

Cyclops was in the center, eyes still shut, with an arm around Storm on one side and Logan on the other. Though he supported them, Storm was directing him, acting as his eyes. He looked as if he was barely keeping them all walking. The professor knew that was exactly the case. Storm was very bruised, and Logan was barely alive. Any other person would have been dead after the beating Magneto had given him.

Jean climbed out and took Storm from Cyclops, helping her into the backseat of the car. Cyclops supported Logan as he got in beside her, then with Jean's guidance he crawled in the other door. Finally Jean got behind the wheel.

In silence they turned and headed for the mansion. There was nothing any of them could say. They had faced the first battle with Magneto and had come up wanting. They were lucky to be alive.

And they had lost Rogue.

Chapter Seventeen

X-Men Mansion

Logan's quarters felt more like a tomb. The school's students were still all asleep, but Storm, Jean, Cyclops, Logan, and the professor were all very much awake.

And Logan was mad. Madder than he had been in a long, long time. He had promised Rogue he would take care of her, then moments later he had been helpless. That ate at him, right in the core of his stomach. He wasn't going to rest until she was back, safe and sound.

Logan stood near the door while Jean and Storm dropped into chairs. Cyclops paced. Logan was becoming more and more disgusted with this Scott Summers kid. And he wasn't real happy with the professor, either.

"You said he wanted me," Logan said, sneering at Xavier, letting the contempt show in his voice.

"I've made a terrible mistake," Xavier admitted, nodding.

"I'd say," Logan said, showing no mercy.

"Magneto's helmet," Xavier said, going on. "It is

somehow designed to block my telepathy. I couldn't see what he was after until it was too late."

"It's not your fault," Cyclops said.

"No?" Logan challenged. "Why blame the biggest brain on the planet?"

"Hey," Cyclops said, turning to face him. "I sure didn't see you stop him."

"How could you, blind man?"

The hotshot's face got red around his visor, and he charged like a bull elephant.

"Scott!" Jean shouted. But it was too late.

Logan laughed and ducked easily under Scott's fist, grabbed his arm, twisted it up behind his back, and slammed the kid into the wall, face first. Then, holding him there, Logan extended a claw right up to the back of Cyclops' head.

"Logan!" Xavier said firmly.

A lock of Cyclops' hair fell to the ground.

Logan flipped Cyclops around and sent him stumbling back. Then he faced the professor, angry and disgusted. "See, it's this kind of thing that makes me wonder how you're gonna outwit Magneto."

With that he turned and slammed open the door. He stormed out into the hall and turned toward the front entrance. As far as he was concerned, he would get Rogue back on his own, or die trying. It was finally something worth dying for.

He started off down the hall.

"What are you doing?"

He stopped and turned to face Storm. Her neck was still bleeding slightly where Sabretooth had held her. And her white hair was streaked with black from the lightning strike she had brought down, very nearly on herself.

"I'm going to find Rogue," Logan said. "What's it look like?"

"You can't just leave," Storm said.

"Why not?" Logan asked. "Should I wait for good old Xavier and his fanatics—you included—to make everything all right?"

"We're not fanatics, Logan," Storm said, her voice low and even and controlled.

"No?" Logan asked, glaring at her. "Then just what are you? Why are you doing all this?"

"Because humanity needs us," Storm said.

Logan took a step back toward her. "Oh, humanity needs you? How have they lived all this time without you?"

"It's a different world now," Storm said, standing face-to-face with him. "As a new species, we have a responsibility to protect them, to teach human beings to accept our presence here."

Logan snorted and turned, then headed into the foyer. Behind him he could hear Storm following. She wasn't going to give up, so in the foyer, near the front door, he turned on her.

"This is what pisses me off about you hypocrites," he said, moving back a step to be right in her face again. "All your high-minded ideals, and you still hate them just as much as they hate you."

She started to object, but he held his hand up for her to stop.

"Look," he said, going on. "I dislike everyone equally, but you . . ." He shook his head in disgust.

"You talk about human beings like they're children, waiting for you to punish them for their ignorance."

He stepped even closer to her, looking her directly in the eye. "They did hate you, didn't they? Hey, it's not like I don't understand." He raised his fist and extended a claw. "They cut open my body and turned me into this. What did they do to you?"

Storm looked flustered, but Logan wouldn't let her turn away. "I've overcome the trials of my past," she finally said.

Logan just sneered at her, retracted his claws, and turned toward the front door.

At the door he glanced back at her. "Good for you."

He started to open the door, then stopped. "You know, I think your professor's right. I think there is a war coming. You sure you're on the right side?"

She looked at him, stiffly refusing to drop her gaze as the silence in the foyer seemed to stretch.

"At least I've chosen a side," she said then.

Again they stared at each other, then, with a shake of his head, he turned and opened the door. Rogue was out there somewhere, and he had to find her. He was wasting his time here.

As he opened the door, Storm gasped.

Standing there in front of him was a man wearing clothes that clearly didn't fit, looking just about as pale and sickly as a man could look and still stand. His clothes were soaked, and a puddle had formed around his feet.

"What the hell happened to you?" Logan asked.

Storm stepped up beside Logan. "Senator Kelly?"

"The Senator Kelly?" Logan asked, actually shocked. "The guy who hates mutants?"

The man nodded, then, very weakly, he said, "I'm looking for Dr. Jean Grey." At that the man's eyes rolled up into his head, showing only whites, and he pitched forward, right into Logan's arms.

It was like holding onto the slime covering a Jell-O mold. Logan barely got him to the ground without dropping him.

"Professor! Jean!" Storm shouted.

Logan stood up. *Well,* he thought, *it looks as if I'm not going anywhere just yet.*

Professor Xavier glanced at the figure lying on the bed as he entered the medical lab. It was clearly the same man who had chaired that hearing just a short time before, yet it wasn't the same man. The man in that hearing had been healthy, cocky, sure in his beliefs. This man looked as if he was burning up with a fever and melting at the same time.

Logan and Storm were standing against a counter on the other side of the bed. Cyclops was sitting on a second medical bed. Jean was standing over the senator.

"So what has happened to him?" Xavier asked her.

Jean shrugged. "I can't explain it, but he's a mutant. Or better put, he's become one."

"What's his mutation?"

"He's extremely adaptable," Jean said. "He can effectively change the shape of his body."

"So why does he look like this?" Logan asked.

"Something's wrong with his mutation," Jean said. "His cells are losing their integrity. They're liquefying. He's literally falling apart."

"Any way to reverse the problem?" Xavier asked.

Jean shook her head.

At that moment the senator moaned and opened his eyes.

Xavier caught fleeting feelings of fear, panic, and extreme anger. He moved his chair up to a position head-high with Senator Kelly as Jean lowered the bed.

"Senator Kelly, my name is Professor Charles Xavier. This is my school."

Kelly nodded. "For mutants?"

Xavier glanced at Jean, then back at Kelly. "Yes."

Kelly half nodded. "I was afraid that if I went to a hospital, they would—"

"Treat you like a mutant?" Xavier said. "We are not what you think. Not all of us."

"Tell that to the ones that did this to me," Kelly said.

Xavier nodded. Then he moved closer and looked directly into the senator's eyes. "I need you to try and relax. I'm not going to hurt you. But I need to find out as best I can what happened to you, to see if we can help you."

Kelly nodded and took as deep a breath as he could.

Xavier looked into the man's eyes, then put a hand on Kelly's wet forehead, letting Kelly's thoughts pour out and into his own mind.

The memories were jumbled, like flashes of light. Xavier was used to it. It was the same with most people. Memories weren't clear, streamlike movies depicting logical sequences of events, but were more like flashbulb images of scenes hooked together, often not even in the right order. And they were always colored heavily with perceptions and feelings.

Flash:

His aide turning into Mystique, her blue face and yellow eyes clear, like the image of a monster. The pain from when she kicked him colored the memory in red.

Thus Magneto had captured the senator. Mystique had done it.

Flash:

Vision fading in and out of pained awakening as Magneto moved into the circle of light, illuminating what looked to be a clearing in a type of cliff-surrounded forest.

Kelly clearly had no idea where he was. And Xavier didn't recognize it either, from anywhere in Magneto's past.

Flash:

Kelly sitting on the chair near a massive machine, fighting to get loose.

Flash:

Magneto rising up inside the machine. He is laughing down at Kelly, toying with him.

Xavier could feel the hatred for Magneto flowing from Kelly. Hatred like nothing he had ever felt before.

Flash:

The light, alive, is crawling over him, through him, inside him.

Flash:

Flash:

Flash:

Extreme bright light and pain, then nothing.

Flash:

Kelly dropping through the air into the ocean.

Xavier pulled back out of the senator's mind as the images began to repeat. He really didn't want or need to see them again.

Or feel that kind of hate again. Once was more than enough to disgust him completely.

Xavier wiped his hands and took a deep breath. It was clear that his old friend was no longer the person he had known.

"Well?" Logan asked as Xavier opened his eyes and wiped his hands again, as if doing that was going to clean away any of the filth he got from the senator's mind. He felt as if he'd touched something really dirty.

He had. The senator was a walking, talking ball of hate and self-loathing, with more disgusting habits and deeds buried in his mind than would be found in a war zone. Losing this man would be no great loss to the world in general.

Xavier was surprised to feel that way.

"Professor?" Jean asked, stepping toward him. "Are you all right?"

He nodded. He was going to be all right as soon as some of the memories went away. "Not here. In my office."

The senator's head lolled to one side, and his eyes closed.

Jean quickly checked him. "He's just sleeping, at least for the moment."

Xavier nodded, then turned his chair toward the door. "Someone needs to stay with him."

"I will," Storm said.

Xavier could hear Logan, Cyclops, and Jean following him.

"Call me if something changes," Jean said.

"I don't think anything will," Xavier said, "at least not for the better."

He meant that in more ways than one.

Chapter Eighteen

Professor Charles Xavier's Office

The mood was different, more focused than it had been, only an hour before. It had been a long night, but Logan was far from tired. All he wanted to do was get Rogue back, and this Senator Kelly had given them their best clue. He was going to stick around until they worked it out. And since the professor had been tap dancing around inside the senator's brain, Logan hoped there would be all sorts of help forthcoming.

"So?" Logan asked as Jean closed the door and the professor moved in behind his desk. "What does Magneto want with Rogue? You get that much?"

"The senator doesn't know," Xavier said.

Logan waited, watching. The professor clearly looked upset by what he had seen and felt in the guy's head. But Logan figured, you go dancing inside any politician's head and you're not going to like what you find.

"It seems that Magneto has built a machine that emits radiation that triggers mutations in normal human beings," Xavier continued. "And it seems to draw its power from Magneto."

"But the mutation is unnatural," Jean said. "Kelly's body is rejecting it. His cells began to break down almost immediately."

"I don't think Magneto knows that," Xavier said. "Kelly escaped before Magneto ran any tests."

"What kind of effect does the radiation have on mutants?" Cyclops asked.

The professor thought for a moment, then said, "None, from what I can tell."

"But it will most likely kill any normal person exposed to it," Jean said, "if Senator Kelly is any indication."

Logan sat, listening, thinking. None of this made any sense. If this Magneto had such a machine, why would he need Rogue? Unless it was to store his own powers.

"Hey, Chuck?" Logan said.

The professor glanced up, and he almost looked annoyed. Logan guessed that no one had called him Chuck in a very long time—if ever.

"You said this machine draws its power from Magneto?"

"Yes," Xavier said.

"What exactly did it do to him?" Logan asked. "Did you get that much from the senator's brain?"

"It clearly weakened him," Xavier said, then paused for what seemed like a very long time. Then he went on. "In fact, it nearly killed him." Sudden awareness swept across his face. "Oh, my God. He's going to transfer his power to Rogue, so next time, the machine kills her—not him."

"And his power will return to him naturally after a short time," Jean said.

Logan froze there, stunned along with the rest. Now

that they knew why Magneto wanted Rogue, the situation seemed even worse. Much worse, actually.

Storm stared in the mirror, dabbing some antiseptic on the scratches on her neck. She was going to be bruised, that was for sure. She was lucky to have come out of that fight with only a few scratches and bruises, and she knew it.

"Is somebody there?" Senator Kelly's voice came weakly from behind her.

She quickly moved over to his bed and smiled down at him, trying to reassure. He was completly covered in viscous fluid, and apparently he could hardly see her. As he moved, water seemed to run from his skin and onto the bed in rivulets.

"Is somebody there?" Kelly asked again.

She picked up his wet, slick hand. "Right here, Senator."

"Are you one of them?" he asked.

"Who is 'them'?" she asked.

"I guess I don't know anymore," he said, and then he actually smiled. Water ran from his face and around his eyes. He didn't even seem to notice.

"I guess it doesn't matter," he added. "Please don't leave."

"All right," Storm said, giving his hand a very gentle squeeze.

"I just don't want to be alone."

"I understand," Storm said. "Very much, actually."

The silence seemed to stretch endlessly, and for a moment Storm thought he had dozed off again.

Then he blinked and focused a little bit, and looked directly at her. "Do you hate normal people?" he asked.

"Sometimes," she said, being honest with him.

"Why?"

She paused for a moment, then decided to give him the straight answer. He deserved that much at least. "I suppose I'm afraid of them."

Kelly laughed, then coughed uncontrollably. She calmed him as best she could.

After a moment he looked up at her again. "Well, I think you've got one less person to be afraid of."

With that he closed his eyes, and his hand tightened around hers. His breathing became shallower and shallower as his hand seemed to be getting smaller and smaller.

So much water was running off of him now that it was dripping in streams onto the floor around the table. The senator was literally melting.

He coughed again, then seemed to settle into the table. His hand continued to shrink in hers, melting away.

She wanted to let go, to go wash, but she stayed. She had promised him she wouldn't leave him alone. She didn't like the man or his beliefs, but no one deserved to die alone.

As she watched, he just got smaller and smaller.

Finally he didn't take another breath.

She was just about to put his hand down when it melted completely, slipping through her fingers.

Logan was getting more and more fed up. It seemed that all they did was talk in circles, and talking wasn't going to get Rogue back. Only action was going to accomplish anything.

"So," Jean said, glancing at Logan, clearly sensing his impatience, "if Magneto wanted to turn a group of people into mutants, where would he do it?"

The question was met with silence. Logan had no idea. Neither, it seemed, did any of them. The target could be any city.

"I'll use Cerebro to try to find Rogue," Xavier said, breaking the silence. "That might help us figure out where they are heading. Cyclops, would you and Storm ready the jet?"

Logan pushed himself away from where he'd been leaning against the wall.

Finally some action.

"Jean," Xavier said, "find Logan a uniform."

"No," Cyclops said. "He's not coming."

Logan turned. His temper flared. "You little—"

"I'm sorry, Professor," Cyclops said, ignoring Logan. "It's not going to happen. He'll endanger the mission and my team."

"Hey," Logan countered, "I wasn't the one who gave the train station a new sunroof. So you can take your mission and stick it. I'll do this on my own."

"Stop acting like children!" Xavier said firmly, looking first at Cyclops, then at Logan. "Both of you! People's lives are at stake. Rogue's life is at stake!"

Logan couldn't even decide how to respond to that.

At that instant the door opened and Storm came in, looking shaken. More shaken than Logan had yet seen her look. She was wiping her hands on a towel, over and over.

"Senator Kelly's dead," Storm said. "He melted. It was not a pleasant thing to watch."

She wiped her hands again.

Silence filled the room again like a thick cloud, holding everything still. Finally Xavier nodded, and moved his chair out from behind his desk and toward the door.

With a quick glance at Cyclops, then Logan, he said, "Settle this."

Then he wheeled himself out of the room.

Professor Xavier wheeled himself into position on the extension ramp leading to Cerebro and let the heavy steel door close behind him. He was angry at both Cyclops and Logan for continuing their petty bickering. And he was worried. Deeply. The images from Senator Kelly kept flashing through his mind. There was no doubt that Magneto thought his device worked, and that he was going to use it on a large number of people, forcing Rogue to act as his stand-in.

The question was where? And when?

Xavier keyed in the commands for Cerebro to track Rogue's brain waves, then wheeled himself into position and put the helmet on his head. They didn't have much time, that he was sure of. He had to find her and find her fast.

As Cerebro started up, he focused on Rogue.

Almost instantly he knew something was wrong.

Horribly wrong.

Sharp pain stabbed through his head, spinning him around and around inside, twisting his thinking, assaulting his mind like a bad nightmare.

He screamed out in pain.

Fighting against losing conciousness, he hit the emergency shut-off switch. Jean had insisted that it be installed on the arm of his chair.

The shut-off switch also triggered alarms and opened the door.

He knew, with a tiny part of what was left of his consciousness, that those things were happening.

But the rest of him was overwhelmed by the pain.

And then the blackness arrived. Creeping, thick blackness, like none he had ever experienced before, slowly filling his awareness.

He wanted to get away from it, but it was inside his head.

He jerked as one more massive jolt of pain shot through his mind. Like a distant object, he could see the light coming in the now-open door. But the light wasn't enough to hold back the darkness.

He pitched forward, out of his chair, out of the helmet.

And the blackness had completely taken him before he hit the floor.

Chapter Nineteen

X-Men Mansion

Cyclops stood over Professor Xavier's body, watching his friend and mentor breathe shallowly. At least he was still breathing. His wheelchair sat next to the bed. Electrodes were taped to his temples and forehead. The monitors showed erratic brain wave activity. Even Cyclops could tell that much.

"What can we do now?" Storm asked.

Jean stood on the other side of the table, and Logan was leaning against the wall behind her. Jean shook her head. "We just have to wait."

Logan looked up. It was clear that Logan was upset, almost as much as the rest of them.

"I think we should get some rest," Jean said. "We're not going to be making very good decisions this tired. We'll take turns watching over the professor."

"And we're going to need to take care of the students," Storm said. "I'll do that."

"Rest," Jean said.

Storm nodded as she headed for the door.

Logan pushed himself away from the wall and moved over to stand by the professor. Then, as he passed by

Cyclops, he put a hand on Cyclops' shoulder. "I'm sorry, Scott."

All Cyclops could do was nod his thanks.

After Storm and Logan had both left, Jean looked at him. "Go rest, then come back and relieve me later in the morning."

"Are you going to be all right here?" Cyclops asked. "You haven't had any rest, either."

Jean looked at the professor. "I'll be fine for four or five hours. I'll wake you if there's any change."

Cyclops kissed her, then headed for the door. Rest didn't seem like it was going to be possible.

And over the next four hours it didn't come easy. But he did manage some sleep, and after a shower and some food he returned to the lab to give Jean a much-needed break. He actually felt better.

After she had left, he moved over and stood above the professor. "You can still hear me, can't you?" he asked.

Of course the professor didn't move. But over the last few hours the monitor had shown some slight stabilizing of his brain waves. Jean had said that that was a good sign.

"I just want to thank you for taking me in," Cyclops said. "Actually, taking us all in."

He stepped back, walked around the table, then continued. "You've taught me everything in my life that is worth knowing. And I want you to know that I'll take care of them."

With that he moved back over to a chair near the monitor and sat down. There was nothing more to say.

And for the moment, nothing more to do.

* * *

After what seemed like an instant nap, but had actually been three hours, Jean showered and returned to the medical lab. Storm and Logan were both there, sitting quietly, waiting. She did a quick check of the professor's vital signs and reported that not only were his brain waves slowly stabilizing, but his vital signs were getting stronger. It was going to take some time, and he wasn't out of the woods yet, but at least he was going in the right direction.

"So what do we do now to save Rogue?" Logan asked. "If it's not too late already."

Jean glanced at the professor. "Well, Cyclops is scanning all news and online reports as we speak, looking for any unusual activity that might give us a clue that something is happening somewhere."

Logan nodded, clearly as satisfied as he could be.

"If one of you would stay with the professor, shift off, and let me know if there are any changes, it would be really helpful."

"You got it," Logan said.

"Gladly," Storm said.

"I'll be in back. I have another idea," Jean said.

She had no idea if she could even fix whatever was wrong with Cerebro. But over the last year she and the professor had worked on the machine a great deal, and she felt she knew it—knew how it worked, and why it worked. If anyone besides the professor could fix it, she could.

It turned out that the main brain had been punctured and broken. Someone had clearly sabotaged it. The questions as to why and how someone could do this would have to wait until later. First she needed to fix it.

Every hour she checked on the professor, then went back to work. Luckily, whoever had sabotaged Cerebro had not known quite what they were doing. The most vital sections had been missed.

Carefully, she replaced wires, tubing, and optic fibers, checking and rechecking every connection to make sure it was not only secure, but correct.

Suddenly, as she connected what seemed to be one of the last optic fibers, Cerebro's brain began to light back up.

Two more optic fibers connected, and the brain's light was as bright as always.

She climbed up out of the harness, moved to the main control board, and ran diagnostic check after diagnostic check. Two hours later, after a few tweaks and one more replaced fiber, everything read completely green.

Cerebro was back and ready, as soon as the professor was well enough to use it.

She started toward the door to tell the others, then realized the full implications of the thoughts that had just run through her mind. It was going to be some time before the professor would be well enough, strong enough, to use Cerebro again. And by that time, Magneto would most certainly have carried out what he was planning.

And Rogue would, from the professor's account of what had happened to Kelly, be only one of the dead. One of hundreds, thousands, perhaps more.

She moved out into the hallway and glanced toward the medical lab. Cyclops and Storm were both leaning against a wall, just outside the lab, waiting. Logan must be inside.

She had to give it a try. There were far too many lives on the line for her to wait.

She turned to the control board as Cyclops looked up and saw her. He started toward her just as she punched the button to close the door.

The last thing she heard from him, as the door locked shut behind her, was, "Jean! No!"

She moved over to the position on the ramp where the professor normally sat and knelt to put her head at the same height. Then she fit Cerebro's helmet over her head and punched in the code on the control panel to search for Rogue's brain waves. She also set the power levels lower than the professor normally used. She had nowhere near the ability he had. Frying her own brain wasn't what she had in mind here.

Faintly through the massive door she could hear Cyclops pounding. She just hoped he didn't do anything stupid like trying to blast through that door. He might be able to do it.

She punched the start switch and then kept her head still as the ramp extended and the walls of the massive round room began to spin.

Suddenly the machine seemed to reach inside her head and grab her brain, clamping down on it like a fist, squeezing harder and harder as the walls around her vanished and her vision floated up and out of the mansion.

She heard herself scream at the pain as the ground sped by under her, until finally she was there, hovering above the tied and gagged Rogue. And instantly, she knew where Magneto was taking her.

The minute that realization was fixed in her mind, Cerebro let her go.

The ramp retracted, the walls slowed and stopped, and the door clicked open to reveal the worried faces of Cyclops, Storm, and Logan. As they came running in, she tried to stand and pitched forward into Cyclops' arms.

"Jean?" Cyclops said, holding her tight. "What have you done?"

She managed to open her eyes and smile up at him with what seemed like her strongest smile, but she wasn't even sure if she'd have the energy to move her lips. Then she managed to choke out, "I've found out where they're going."

Then she closed her eyes again. It was just too much work to keep them open.

Chapter Twenty

Liberty Island—New York City

The entire harbor around Ellis and Liberty Islands crawled with security as the leaders of every major nation gathered for the opening ceremonies of the international peace conference to be held on Ellis Island.

The night was lit with spotlights, and the water was dotted with police boats. Underwater sensors guarded the islands, and three different security satellites provided constant surveillance of the entire area. The U.S. Secret Service and the FBI were responsible for all the world leaders' security, working with each government's security agency. As far as they were all concerned, not even a fly could get near these leaders without them knowing about it.

Liberty Island ground security had been given over to almost fifty of New York's finest, patrolling on a constant basis. Both the FBI and the Secret Service had command posts set up on the side of Liberty Island that faced Ellis Island, where the opening ceremonies would take place.

The line of limos jammed the one road to Ellis Island like a traffic jam at rush hour. The backup, of course, was exacerbated by the intense security check each car had to go through just to get to the island.

On the dock side of Liberty Island, away from Ellis Island, a New York cop named Mike walked a set path. He was in his thirties, and was pretty much disgusted at the night duty he'd been forced to pull because of all the big shots in limos. He would much rather have been home watching a game on television, or sitting at Henry's tavern, downing a few beers. Instead he walked a very short, very monotonous beat of less than a hundred paces on Liberty Island.

Mike was so focused on his cold hands that he didn't see the mutant on the stone ledge above him, didn't hear Toad jump, didn't even know what hit him when Toad crushed him flat, killing him instantly.

Another cop named Stan, on the next beat over, thought he might have heard a crunch at the time Mike's bones were being smashed, but he couldn't see anything.

Two minutes later, Stan met the same fate.

In the water just beyond the dock, a New York City police boat slowly moved toward the Liberty Island dock. The pilot was a man in his forties, standing behind the open wheel, taking the boat carefully in.

On the dock another cop named Hank waved.

The pilot waved back.

Then Hank waved again, this time with his entire body, his mouth open in a silent scream of shock as Sabretooth ran him through, then picked him up. A moment later Sabretooth tossed Hank's body over the side of the dock and moved back into the shadows, to take care of any other police who might come near the dock at any point in the near future.

On the boat the pilot started to shift, changing quickly into Mystique. At her feet the original pilot lay dead, his open eyes staring up at her. On the back deck of the boat, under a heavy tarp, rested the machine that would shortly change the world forever.

The boat bumped gently into the dock, and Mystique moved to quickly tie it off. Then she turned and said, "Clear."

Magneto came up from below, followed a safe distance behind by Rogue. She was wrapped in a tight-fitting jacket, her hands tied together, a metal collar around her neck so Magneto could control her completely.

He stepped up on the deck and took a deep breath of the cold bay air, then looked up at the Statue of Liberty towering above them. "Isn't it magnificent?"

"I've seen it," Rogue said.

Magneto took off his helmet and held it under his arm, then looked back up at the statue. "I first saw her in 1949. America was going to be the land of tolerance. Of peace."

Sabretooth jumped down onto the deck and helped Mystique uncover the machine.

"Are you going to kill me?" Rogue asked.

Magneto looked from the statue to her, then nodded. "Yes."

"Why?" Rogue asked.

"Because there is no land of tolerance," Magneto replied. "There is no land of peace." He pointed up at the Liberty statue. "Not here, not anywhere."

"I'm sure the professor doesn't agree with you on that," Rogue said.

"True," Magneto said. "But Charles has not seen what I've seen. Women and children, whole families, destroyed simply because they were born different from those in power. Well, after tonight, the world's powerful will be just like us. They will return home as brothers, as mutants. And our cause will be theirs. Your sacrifice will mean our survival."

"I'm thrilled," she said.

"Granted, I understand that is a small consolation to the likes of you," Magneto said. Then he turned. "Put her in the machine."

He stepped off the boat and looked up at the statue. "Tell me when she's ready, and I'll raise the machine up into the torch."

X-Men Mansion

Logan packed the clothes Xavier had given him into a duffel bag. They were the only clothes he had at the moment, since his camper had been destroyed. And now that he knew where Magneto was going to attack, he was headed there, to save Rogue if he could.

More than likely he was going to die trying, but he had faced death so many times already that it made very little difference to him. He had promised her, and he was going to do his best to keep that promise.

Storm knocked lightly and stepped into the room.

"What?" Logan asked, not looking up at her.

"Cyclops said he would like to see everyone down in the map room."

"Yeah?" he asked.

"Everyone," she said.

He nodded. So the kid was finally starting to do what Xavier seemed to think he could do. Take charge.

Storm turned and headed down the hall. Logan tossed the bag on the bed and followed. Might as well see what Sunglasses Boy was planning. That way they wouldn't get in each other's way.

The map room was something Logan hadn't seen in action before. It, too, was a round room, with a large, round table in the center. Control panels lined the sides.

At the moment, the table was covered with a very detailed holographic image of the New York City area, focusing on the bay with Liberty and Ellis Islands. The three-dimensional Statue of Liberty was startling to look at. Logan was impressed. They never seemed to be lacking the latest gadget.

On the board he saw dots of different colors. Jean nodded to him, then pointed at one of the dots. "Red shows New York cop foot patrols. Blue shows the current location of police and other security boats."

He nodded. This was one very, very sophisticated map. Clearly it was being fed by a direct link to a satellite of some sort. The professor spared no expense for his team.

When Storm and Logan stepped up to the map, Cyclops was studying it with intense care. Finally, without looking up he said, "All right, we can go in here, at the George Washington Bridge."

Cyclops moved a control ball on the control panel in front of him, and the map shifted, following the motion of a jet coming in low under the bridge.

"We come around the bank just off of Manhattan," Cyclops went on, giving commentary that followed the motion on the map. "We land on the far side of Liberty Island. Here."

The map showed the point where they would hit the island. Patrols were light on that side. Actually, they seemed too light. But Logan didn't mention that.

For a moment they all stood there in silence. It was clear to him that he was going to have a much better shot getting to Rogue if he went with this group. And just maybe they could all get out of it alive.

"So what about radar?" he asked.

Cyclops glanced up and actually smiled. "If they have anything that can pick up our jet, they deserve to catch us."

Logan nodded. "Good enough." Then he pointed at the place where they intended to land. "Doesn't that look a little light on the guard numbers?"

Cyclops studied the area again, nodding slowly. As he watched, another red dot showing a New York cop winked out.

"It seems," Cyclops said, "that Magneto is ahead of us. We leave in ten minutes, people." At that he turned and headed for the door, without looking back.

Logan moved with Storm into the ready room off the hangar. He glanced at the uniforms, then shook his head and started for the jet.

"Hold on a second," Cyclops said, strolling into the room and stepping right up to Logan. "We do this, we do it as a team. Are you going to have a problem taking orders?"

Logan stared into the visor of the man facing him. The guy knew Logan could cut him down in an instant, yet he had the guts to stand up to him like this. Challenge him. The guy had courage, Logan had to hand him that.

"I don't know," Logan said. "Give me an order."

They continued to stare at each other for a moment, then Cyclops turned and moved to his locker. He grabbed a uniform and tossed it at him. "Put it on."

Logan caught the black uniform and nodded, following Cyclops' order, trying not to smile.

Chapter Twenty-one

New York Harbor

The night was cold, star filled, and moonless. The lights of Manhattan and the surrounding cities and towns shone like bright, twinkling stars that framed the blackness of the bay and rivers.

Cyclops surveyed the jet's instruments, making sure everything was in perfect working order. Ahead he could see the George Washington Bridge, and beyond it Liberty Island was lit up, the statue dominating the bay. The line of cars stretching out to Ellis Island seemed to have stopped. Or if it was moving, it was so slow that Cyclops couldn't see it from their current height of three thousand feet, even with the monitors.

Beside him, Storm studied other screens. And in the next two seats back, Jean and Logan waited. Shortly after they had taken off, Logan had extended his claws—to customize the gloves of his new costume. Otherwise the short flight had been tensely silent.

"All right," Cyclops said, "there's the bridge. I'm taking us in. Storm, some cover please."

"You got it," Storm said. Her eyes went milky white.

As if to mirror those eyes, below, around, and under the G.W. Bridge a cloud of fog began to form over the calm, cold water. Cyclops watched as it began rolling down the Hudson River, past midtown Manhattan, then out toward Liberty Island.

He took the jet down quickly, almost in a straight dive, dropping to just forty feet over the water and skimming along in silent mode.

"You could warn a fella you're going to make a move like that," Logan said.

Cyclops glanced back and smiled wryly at the strained expression Logan wore. He was gripping the armrest tightly. "Not a good flyer, huh?" Scott asked.

"I can't remember," Logan said.

"Got me, too," Storm admitted.

"Sorry," Cyclops said, still smiling. "I'll warn you both next time."

"Thanks," Logan said.

And somehow, Cyclops knew he was sincere.

"Going to tactical," Storm announced as they entered the fog right under the bridge.

The windows seemed to darken slightly, then, as if it had turned to daylight, the view of the surrounding area shifted to startling clarity.

"Amazing stuff," Logan said.

"Highly advanced version of infrared night vision," Storm said. "Makes darkness a thing of the past."

"I'll say," Logan said.

They reached the bay, and Cyclops slowed the jet down, almost into hover mode, moving slowly toward the far side of Liberty Island. There was no point in trying to save a few seconds at this point, or in drawing attention to themselves. It was far better they got there without being seen at all.

Ellis Island

Craig Downer, a seven-year veteran of the Secret Service, stood on a tower overlooking the events unfolding below. He was in charge of a small squad of six agents, and each squad commander reported to a superior. It wasn't often that the Secret Service broke down into squads like this, but given the size of this particular event, it was the best way to keep track of everything and everyone.

At the moment the U.S. Navy band was playing a selection of different music from various countries. The bandstand was set up to the west of the main stage area. The music seemed to echo over the water, and to Craig it seemed out of tune more than anything else.

A bank of translators filled large booths that had been set up just below his tower. They were constantly speaking into a bank of microphones as the main public address system announced each head of state, each dignitary, as he or she arrived.

Out over the water, the lights of the patrol boats moved in a constant pattern that over the last few hours had become familiar. Then suddenly, as he was just about to turn away, he thought he caught a glimpse of something large and black blocking a portion of the distant shore lights, moving about forty feet above the water.

He keyed his mike. "Can I get confirmation that harbor airspace has been cleared?"

"Roger that," a voice responded. "Nothing moving over three feet above that water. Airline flights have been shifted to the north approaches, as well."

"Thanks," Craig said, staring intently at the area where he thought he'd seen the black form.

Nothing.

He scanned the horizon along the lit shoreline, all the way to the Statue of Liberty.

Nothing.

Maybe he was just getting too paranoid for his own good. He was starting to imagine things. And in his job, that wasn't a good thing to do.

He went back to scanning the road that led onto Ellis Island, and all the stretch limos still waiting to be cleared. This was going to be a long night before it was over. A very long night.

Liberty Island

Magneto stared out of one of the observation windows set in the head of the Statue of Liberty, watching the lights on the distant Ellis Island. Behind him Sabretooth paced, back and forth, his footsteps echoing in the metal space. Except for the pacing, the silent statue felt like a tomb.

The two cops stationed in the torch above were dead, as was every person who had had the misfortune of being stationed inside the statue. Magneto deeply regretted having needed to take innocent lives like that, but he had had no alternative. The survival of an entire race came first.

After a moment, he keyed in the radio mike that connected him to Mystique, who was located in the main area in the statue's base. She was stationed at a police monitor that showed all the activities on Ellis Island. "How long?"

Her voice came back clear. "Ten minutes until curtain."

Outside, a dense fog was rolling in over Liberty Island. That was odd. It took him a moment before he realized why it was odd.

He keyed his mike again, this time to everyone on his team. "Stay sharp, people. We're not alone." He smiled, then thought, *You're too late, Charles.*

He got no response.

Sabretooth stepped up beside Magneto and looked out the window. Then he growled like a dog at an intruder, and turned to leave.

"Stay here," Magneto ordered.

"But—"

"I need you with me," Magneto said. "Once I've given my powers to the girl, I'll be temporarily weakened. You will be my only defense."

Sabretooth nodded and moved back to the other side of the statue's head, where the stairs curved up. He was following orders, but Magneto could tell he wasn't happy about it.

Ellis Island

Craig Downer got the message clearly through his earpiece. "John Henry has arrived."

John Henry was the code name assigned to the president and his party. Craig and the rest of his people were here to protect everyone, but as always, their first priority was the president.

"Ladies and Gentlemen," the public address system announced. "The president and first lady of the United States of America."

On the red carpet leading into the main area, Craig could see the president and his wife walking, smiling, waving to the cheering crowds. They were surrounded by a full contingent of Secret Service. And a dozen more were scattered up through the crowd ahead of them.

Craig scanned along the road, scanned the crowds in front of the president, and then, as the president and first lady got to their seats, he looked out over the black water where he had seen the shape. The Statue of Liberty stood out there, brightly lit and standing guard over the bay.

There was something odd about old lady Liberty. He couldn't put his finger on it.

Craig shook his head. Why was he having such a bad feeling about all of this?

So far everything had gone smoothly.

Maybe that was worrying him. Maybe it had gone too smoothly.

Chapter
Twenty-two

Liberty Island

Logan breathed an inward sigh of relief as Cyclops brought the jet down smoothly into the water and cut the engines. The sensation shifted to the gentle rocking action of water as the engine ports closed up to function like pontoons.

Cyclops climbed out onto the wing and jumped to a nearby rock, using special cords to secure the jet in place. Inflatable black buffers protected it from striking the rocks. With luck, they were going to need the jet to get away. And more than likely, it was going to have to be a fast exit.

Logan followed Cyclops out, then helped Jean and Storm reach dry land while Cyclops finished securing the jet. Logan couldn't sense any motion or detect the scent of anyone in the immediate vicinity, but that didn't necessarily mean anything. Their enemies had shown remarkable ability when it came to masking their presence.

He and Storm took up positions on the hill, waiting there until Cyclops and Jean joined them. Storm's fog was thick and heavy, and the air had turned cold and biting. Above them Logan could see the Statue of Liberty towering against a backdrop of the night's blackness, all lit up with spotlights that cut through the fog. Across the bay he could see the gathering on Ellis Island, and he could hear the faint sounds of the music drifting out over the waves.

"Take a look at this," Storm said from her position to his right as Jean and Cyclops joined them. She was indicating a huge, green, rounded object composed entirely of metal.

At first Logan couldn't tell what it was exactly.

"The base of the torch," Jean said, looking up. There was a hint of awe in her voice. "Can you believe that?"

It finally dawned on Logan just what she was talking about. Above them, he could see that the base of Liberty's torch had been removed—replaced, more than likely, with the base of the machine that Senator Kelly had described to the professor.

"Spread out and head for the main entrance," Cyclops said. "Logan, take point."

"Got it," Logan acknowledged.

Twenty feet farther up the rocks, under a stone wall, he came across the first body. The cop had practically been gutted, and from the look on his face, he hadn't died easily or quickly. Logan could smell the scent of Sabretooth on the guy.

Two more policemens' bodies had been tossed behind the bushes near the main entrance. Logan waited there, in the shadows, as Jean, Storm, and then Cyclops came up out of the darkness, appearing like ghosts, moving silently and quickly. Logan had to admit the professor had trained them well. They were functioning like commandos.

"Two bodies," Logan said, pointing into the bush behind him.

Cyclops nodded. "Jean, keep scanning ahead. You and I are now on point. Logan, stay close to Storm. Watch her back."

"Copy that," Logan said.

So far the kid was acting like a real commander. And so far his orders all made sense. He was going to owe Scott an apology if they both got out of this alive.

Cyclops went in the right double door and continued right.

Jean took the left door and went left.

A moment later Cyclops' voice said, "Clear."

Storm and Logan moved toward the front doors the same way as Cyclops and Jean. As they entered, Storm clipped her cape to her wrists, keeping it closer to her body.

Passing through the doorway, Logan set off a metal detector. With a look of disgust, he popped his claws and plunged them into the machine, putting a stop to the strident alarm.

The inside of the statue's main foyer boasted a girdered ceiling, then a long hallway heading toward the center of the structure. There was an empty security desk to one side and a metal detector blocking much of the entrance.

Logan went around it on the right.

Storm on the left.

The two cops who had been manning this area were bleeding behind the desk, their throats cut cleanly, their blood so fresh it wasn't yet drawing flies.

A six-foot replica of the statue stood guard on one side of the hallway about halfway down. As Logan went past it, he paused. A few feet farther on, he whispered to Cyclops. "There's someone here."

"Where?" Cyclops asked.

"I don't know," Logan said. "Keep your eyes open."

They continued down the long hallway—slowly, carefully—to where it opened into a two-tiered museum.

The sense was becoming even stronger. Logan glanced around. Still nothing. They reached the center area that stretched upward into the body of the statue. There they stopped, surrounded by displays and side rooms, with a railing curving above them, concealing a dark balcony.

Cyclops gestured, and they spread out, keeping under the overhang of the balcony.

Finally, Logan couldn't stand it any longer—the sense that someone was just behind them. "Hang on," he said to Cyclops, who nodded.

Logan headed toward the front entrance, moving quickly and silently.

Nothing.

He was about to turn back when he heard Cyclops' voice down the hallway.

"Anything?" Cyclops asked.

"I know there's someone here," a voice responded. A voice that sounded exactly like his own. "But I can't see them."

At that he broke into a sprint, as fast as he could move, back down the hall toward the others.

Someone, or something, who looked, dressed, and sounded exactly as he did, was standing in front of

Cyclops. Then the imposter extended his claws and went to swipe at the unsuspecting X-Man.

Logan leaped and tackled the doppelganger, square in the back, sending them both tumbling head over heels into the steel wall, then into a side room cluttered with exhibits.

Recovering from his surprise, Cyclops focused on both of them as they came up, facing each other. Logan glanced at Scott. "Wait."

The imposter did the same thing.

Said the same thing.

Suddenly a massive metal door slammed down into place, cutting off Logan and the imposter from the others.

Logan spun for an instant, then turned back. But the imposter was gone.

Mystique. The blue woman was a fighting expert and could change her form at will.

Then the lights cut out.

"Ah, crap," Logan said. He was certain he knew what was going to happen next.

And he was right. A boot slammed into his face, sending him crashing over backward.

He came up ready to fight, his claws fully extended, using all his heightened senses to figure out where his opponent might be lurking.

The blackness seemed almost too black.

A whisper of movement caused him to turn, just in time to roll with another blow to the head. This time the impact sent him crashing into a glass display case.

He rolled again and came up, moving toward the

far wall. There he found a switch and turned it on, bringing the lights back up. He was in a gift shop.

Mystique was nowhere to be seen. Yet he still could sense her presence. He moved slowly, with animal grace, turning, employing every sense. She had to breathe, so he listened. She had a faint smell, so he let his nose guide him.

He glided toward one side of the small gift shop.

Suddenly a mirror behind him seemed to move, and he slashed at it with his claws, smashing the glass.

But it had been a reflection.

Then the steel door flew open, and a shadow darted out into the main area.

"Blast, blast, *blast,*" he said, following her.

Jean stood beside Cyclops as he prepared to blast down the door that separated them from Logan and Mystique. Suddenly there was a sickening thud as Toad dropped from the balcony, bounced once, and kicked Cyclops hard in the side, sending him crashing head over heels into another side room.

Instantly the metal door to that room slammed down, cutting her off from Cyclops.

"Jean, watch out!" Storm shouted.

Jean twisted around to discover Toad, facing her head-on. His tongue shot out and struck her face, coating her with a slimy substance that congealed almost instantly.

He laughed. "Hate to kiss and run."

It took Jean only a moment to realize that she couldn't breathe. The stuff was blocking her nose and mouth. She clawed at it, fighting to free herself of it.

An instant later the metal door that had slammed down on Cyclops melted under the heat of his energy beam. Scott came tearing out, firing at Toad, who dodged out of the way, ricocheting off two walls, gaining the momentum he needed to kick Cyclops back into the room he'd just escaped from.

Then Storm attacked him, and he rolled over, finding the leverage to knock her up and over the railing into the balcony area.

Then Cyclops was back, and Toad leaped up and out of sight, also on the balcony.

Jean was starting to black out. She dropped to her knees, then to her back, fighting the stuff that clung to her face, her throat, and her nose. It had hardened until it felt like bone, completely blocking her air.

"Jean!" Cyclops said, bending over her. "Hold still!"

He desperately tried to pry it off, but it would not yield.

She could feel the blackness coming in around her. She desperately needed air. She fought to keep her eyes open.

Finally Cyclops stood. "Jean! Stop moving!"

She didn't understand.

"Stop moving!" he shouted.

She did as he ordered.

He fired an incredibly thin, extraordinarily focused beam of energy from his visor. It struck the slime that had crusted over her face. The energy smashed it to pieces.

Jean gulped in a sweet breath of wonderful air as Cyclops bent over her, holding her.

She held him back as hard as she could.

That had been just too close.

*   *   *

Storm moved quietly along the exhibits, searching for Toad. He was up here somewhere, and she was going to find him.

And kick his tail right out to sea.

As she came out from behind a display case, she heard the elevator doors open. She glanced that way, only to find the doors were standing open on an empty shaft.

What was going on?

Suddenly, something dripped on her from above.

She tried to duck but wasn't in time. Toad swung down and kicked her squarely, sending her careening across the floor. An instant later he was on top of her, his scaly hands touching her face, his legs pinning her arms.

"Such pretty skin," he sneered, caressing her cheek. She fought a wave of revulsion. "So perfect. I guess some mutants were just born lucky."

Storm kicked him in the back of the head. Then, as he moved, she wrenched an arm free and drove a fist squarely into his ugly face.

It was like punching a marshmallow covered with scales.

Instantly he leaped back up into the rafters.

"Nice try," he said mockingly, "but you're going to have to do better than that."

She scrambled to her feet, ready to fight, as he swung through the rafters like a gymnast on a high bar, using the force of one such swing to kick her hard, right in the chest.

The blow knocked the air out of her.

She flew backward through the air and smashed directly into the back of the open elevator shaft.

Her head connected with the wall with a resounding *crack*.

The impact hurt worse than almost anything she'd ever experienced.

An instant later, she dropped into the darkness.

Chapter
Twenty-three

Liberty Island

Toad perched on the railing, watching the two mutants below. The one he had slimed was still alive, thanks to the mutant with the visor. But that wouldn't be the case for long.

He lined up, ready to drop on both of them at once. Sort of a two-birds-with-one-drop kind of thing. The sound of their bones crunching under the impact was going to be wonderful. With luck some of their brains and guts would squirt out—like someone stepping on a tube of toothpaste.

He loved it when that happened.

Behind him the elevator doors opened.

He twisted around just as wind blew up through the elevator shaft, increasing in intensity, rattling the doors, then knocking over tourist displays.

Slowly floating upward on the wind, the mutant with the white hair and the smooth skin rose into view.

"Don't you people ever die?" he complained, jumping down from the railing to face her.

At that the wind around him picked up violently.

Displays and merchandise began flying toward him, striking him.

The woman had cuts on her forehead, and her arms were bleeding. Her eyes were solid white, shining like lasers, staring at him. Her expression spoke volumes, and Toad began to wonder if he should find a convenient escape route.

"Don't like being dropped down an elevator shaft, huh?" he asked, shouting bravado into the wind as he used his webbed feet to hold himself to the floor. Slowly, even as the wind increased, he inched closer to her, never letting the smile slip from his face. When he reached her she was going to be sorry she had even tried to mess with him.

His opponent's white eyes opened even wider, and the winds increased, pushing beyond hurricane force. Now he found himself slipping, moving backward, no matter how firmly he tried to hold on with his sticky feet.

Suddenly, a counter appeared and knocked against his leg, and his feet went out from under him.

He grabbed the carpet with his hands, but it ripped, sending him tumbling into the air and out a large window that opened onto an observation deck.

Beyond that, only the dark, open ocean waited for him.

But this white-haired witch wasn't going to get the best of him yet.

He lashed out with his tongue, grabbing the railing of the observation deck, holding on, flapping in the hard wind like a flag in a breeze. His strength could outlast hers, he was sure of that. She had to tire soon, then he would kill her. And take pleasure in doing it.

The glass on the doors exploded outward as the white-haired mutant walked out onto the observation deck, rising off the ground, buoyed by the winds she summoned around her.

She didn't look tired.

Then she raised her arms.

The air around Toad began to crackle and pop. He could feel the hairs on his head standing up even in the wind.

"Do you know what happens to a toad when it gets hit by lightning?" she shouted.

The pain in his tongue was intense as a massive bolt of lightning struck the railing. The jolt of electricity moved up his tongue and tore through his body.

The last thing he remembered was flying on the wind far, far above the dark ocean, his now-worthless tongue trailing behind him like the tail of a kite.

Then he blacked out. Luckily, this occurred before he hit the very hard surface of the water.

Back on the balcony, the wind died down and Storm smiled. "Same thing that happens to everything else," she said, answering her own question.

"Same old thing."

Logan moved quickly down the hallway, keeping all his senses alert. He knew Mystique was close by, but where? And how was she going to attack?

Suddenly Storm burst through the doors just in front of him. "Is that you?" she asked, looking him over carefully.

Logan moved up close to her. "Shh, the other one ain't far away."

His nose caught the now-familiar odor.

Storm nodded. "Come on. We need to regroup."

"I know," Logan said, "but there's a problem."

As fast as he could move, he grabbed Storm's wrist and yanked it up. There were three claws protruding from her wrist. Claws she had planned on using to run him through.

The claws reverted back as Mystique's blue hand returned to its natural shape. Logan spun and struck out with his elbow, smashing her square in the nose as hard as he could.

She went down like a sack of flour. She wasn't going to be moving again for a long, long time.

And it was going to take all her changing ability to fix what was left of her nose.

"Always remember," he said, standing over her limp, blue body, "no two women smell alike."

He turned and headed back to the main area of the museum.

As he entered the center room, Cyclops and Jean spun and took up defensive positions.

"It's me," Logan said, striding toward them.

"Prove it," Cyclops said.

"You're a jerk," Logan said, smiling at their visor-eyed leader.

Cyclops paused for a moment, then nodded and smiled. "Okay. Let's find Storm."

"Right here," she said.

Logan glanced at where she stood on the balcony, clearly tired, and bleeding in a number of places.

"You all right?" Jean asked.

"Better than Toad," Storm said, and smiled.

"And you're much better looking, too," Logan said.

"You sure know how to make a beat-up woman feel better," Storm said wryly.

"Okay then," Cyclops said. "Two down and two to go."

"Why do I think the next two are going to be the hardest?" Logan said.

"Because you're right," Cyclops replied.

Chapter Twenty-four

Liberty Island

The statue's interior was lit with a few strategically placed spotlights; the stairs had lights directly over them. It was a long climb, but it didn't take much time for Logan, with Cyclops directly behind him, to reach the upper platform. Stairs led off in two directions: one into the arm, and the other up into the head. The door that led into the arm was closed and locked tight. Looking down, Logan could see all the latticework of the statue's body. Above, the opening stretched into the head.

"Looks like Magneto's got the arm blocked," Storm said, pointing at the door on one side of the platform.

"Can you blast through it?" Logan asked Cyclops.

"Not without tearing the whole arm off," Cyclops said.

Above them, Logan could hear the sound of wind coming from the head of the statue. Maybe there was a way to the arm from there. He glanced up, then at Cyclops, who caught the meaning and nodded.

"Follow me," Cyclops said, heading up.

They all came up onto the platform inside the head

and scattered, ready for anything. The inside walls of the head and face were covered with metal support beams and more latticework. Stairs continued up to observation platforms in the statue's crown.

Suddenly, Logan found that he couldn't move. It was as if his legs were glued to the floor, his arms frozen in the air.

Magneto!

"Get out of here," he said to the others. "Quick!"

"What's wrong?" Cyclops asked.

"I can't move," Logan said.

In the next instant, he was shoved hard, back against a wall. His fists were brought up and pushed into his chest, so that if he extended his claws he would stab himself.

A band of metal curled up and wrapped around him, pinning his fists to his chest. He tried to shove against the band, but it held him tight.

Then the room erupted into something from a bad cartoon nightmare as the metal bracing from the wall tore loose and flew everywhere, dancing, attacking, as if each piece had a life of its own.

Cyclops managed to blast a few of the braces, but there were just too many. One came up from behind and wrapped around his neck, forcing his head back and pulling him to the wall.

Storm and Jean were both caught as well and yanked to the wall.

The metal shoved Jean face-to-face with Cyclops. Then two metal spikes came in and locked Cyclops' head in place.

Storm looked more angry than Logan had ever

seen her as four bands bent and pinned her to a wall near him.

Then, from the hole in the top of the statue's head, Magneto floated down, using the magnetic pull to support himself, landing gently in the middle of the room. He was wearing a smile that spoke of arrogant confidence.

"Welcome, my friends," he said.

Sabretooth thumped down behind him. Logan noticed that his dog tags were hanging around Sabretooth's neck. If it was the last thing he did, he was going to get those back.

Sabretooth moved over to where Jean and Cyclops were locked against the wall.

"You'd better close your eyes," Magneto warned the young team leader.

At that, Sabretooth ripped Cyclops' visor off his head and put it in his pocket. Fortunately, Cyclops had heeded the warning, though Logan knew that if he opened his eyes in the slightest, he would destroy everything that lay in front of him—including Jean.

Magneto laughed, then turned to Logan. "And I'm so glad you could make it."

Logan's only response was a growl.

"Storm, fry him," Cyclops shouted.

Magneto laughed. "By all means. A bolt of lightning into a huge copper conductor. I thought you lived at a school."

With that, Magneto stepped to the center of the platform and spoke into a radio. "Mystique? Mystique, where are you?"

Logan knew Magneto wasn't going to be getting an answer anytime soon, but said nothing. Magneto lowered the radio and tossed it to Sabretooth. "Find one of the security bands, and then find out if the ceremonies have started yet."

"You can't do this," Jean said. "I've seen Senator Kelly."

"Ah," Magneto said, nodding, "so the good senator survived his fall? And the swim to shore? He's more powerful than I could have possibly imagined."

"Kelly's dead," Jean said. "His body rejected the mutation and he simply melted. His cells fell apart."

"No, that's not possible," Magneto said, a hint of uncertainty in his voice. He glared at her.

"It happened," Jean said flatly.

Magneto began to pace back and forth, saying nothing.

Logan could see that the news had shaken the man. Then, suddenly, Magneto stopped and turned on Jean. "Can't you see what I'm trying to do? Why do you stand in my way?"

"Because you're going to kill thousands of people," Jean said simply.

But Magneto shook it off. Clearly, he refused to accept her claims about Senator Kelly. Instead he said, "I'm doing this for you. I'm doing this to put an end to the persecution of my people."

"Bull!" Logan spat.

Magneto turned and pinned him with a stare. But Logan refused to give in.

"One of your people is about to get fried in your little flawed machine. I bet she's feeling pretty persecuted, pal. If you were so righteous, it'd be you in that thing."

"Oh, yes?" Magneto asked, looking at Logan. "Who would lead them then? You? Charles?"

He turned and faced Jean again. "This is not the time for politics and debate. It is time for strength. Our people will need leadership."

"Sure," Logan said, planting as much disgust in his voice as he could. "All hail Magneto, king of the new race and all-around genocidal maniac." He laughed. "You know, I remember my history, and that sounds awfully familiar, don't you think?"

Magneto glared at Logan as the radio in Sabretooth's hand crackled.

"Boss?" Sabretooth said.

Magneto turned as Sabretooth held up the radio. "Tapped in on one of their bands."

Magneto nodded as the radio came to life. Even from a distance, Logan could hear what the Secret Service guy was saying, unaware that his security had been compromised. "The house is full. Repeat, the house is full. Proceed to phase two."

Magneto nodded. "It seems the party next door is under way. It's time."

He glanced around at Jean and Cyclops, then back at Logan. "Good-bye, brothers."

With that, he floated up through the hole in the head of the statue.

Logan twisted, trying to fight his way out of the steel belt that held him, without luck.

Sabretooth just sneered at him.

More than anything else in the world, Logan wanted to wipe that sneer right off his ugly face.

Chapter
Twenty-five

Ellis Island

Secret Service agent Craig Downer scanned the crowds milling about below his tower, then he looked out over the water toward Liberty Island again. He'd just been informed that they were having radio trouble, and communications were down for the entire city police contingent on the island. Nonetheless, he'd been assured that it would be fixed shortly. *It had better be,* he mused pessimistically. Four Secret Service agents were headed there now by boat to check the situation out. He didn't dare take any chances.

Down at ground level, the UN secretary general was finishing his speech.

"We must never forget," the secretary general said, "that the welfare of the smallest person, in the remotest corner of the world, is connected by infinite links to that of the world's leaders, gathered here today. The alliance of the world is coming, and tonight we have taken the first steps."

Polite applause filled the air.

At that moment the fireworks started. Red and green streamers shot into the air, the explosions echoing over the water. The display was scheduled to last for six minutes—six very long minutes as far as Downer was concerned.

He continued to scan the crowd and the distant Statue of Liberty, now illuminated even more with the blues and reds and greens of the fireworks.

Something was wrong. He could sense it.

He just didn't know what it was, and calling an emergency based only on his gut wasn't something he could do—not on a night as important as this one.

So he stood, watched, and stayed very alert.

Liberty Island

Logan watched carefully as Sabretooth moved to one of the observation windows in the statue's head to watch the fireworks exploding out over the water. It was going to be now or never.

He took a deep breath. This was going to hurt. But pain was something he had experienced a lot of in the past. He would survive this.

As hard and as fast as he could, he extended the claw of his right index finger.

It shot through his chest with a stabbing pain and made him suck in his breath. The claw went out his back and into the steel band holding him.

Quickly, using his entire body for leverage, he twisted, cutting the band. As he fell forward, he withdrew the claw, growling as pain again waved through his body, twisting him, bending him over for a moment.

But he was free.

And as always, his wound was healing quickly.

Sabretooth spun around and roared when he saw what Logan had done.

"Glad to see me, huh?" Logan said, and before Sabretooth could react, he charged. With a flying kick, Logan planted one foot in his opponent's stomach, the other on his shoulder, and sprang upward, using Sabretooth as a springboard that allowed him to get up and out, to the observation area on the statue's crown.

With one clean motion, he landed and rolled, then braced himself and looked around. The arm was too far away for him to reach. And he couldn't see anything going on up there yet.

"What the hell do I do now?" he asked himself.

At that instant, Sabretooth shot up through the hole in the statue and smashed into Logan at full tilt, sending him over the crown of the statue and onto the spikes of the headpiece.

It seemed his question had been answered for him.

Logan rolled and came up fast as Sabretooth charged.

"Here kitty, kitty, kitty," Logan mocked, crouched and waiting. "Come and get what you deserve."

Rogue, for the past half hour, had been struggling to loosen the cuffs that bound her to Magneto's machine. Her wrists were raw and bleeding, and the panel near her feet had been dented by her kicks, but she had made no real progress at all.

Now fireworks had started out over the water. She knew time must be short. Very short.

Magneto stepped in through the door that led from the observation area into the torch, where Rogue was being held. He was smiling.

"No," Rogue said. "Please don't do this."

"I'm sorry, my dear," Magneto said.

He didn't look sorry at all. He actually looked excited, like a child on his birthday. She watched as he removed his gloves, then took a few deep breaths, as if he were getting ready to jump into a deep pool.

Then he moved up to her, his cold eyes locking with hers. She tried to turn away, tried to pull her hands loose, but she couldn't.

With his bare hands, he touched her face.

Suddenly she felt the incredible energy flowing into her.

She could see everything that he had seen.

She knew what he knew.

She saw all the death, all the horror.

Abruptly, he let go and staggered backward, his face white with shock. The machine around her came to life, shifting, yanking her hands down onto the handles. The rings began to spin, slowly at first, then faster.

She fought hard to let go, trying to use his power, his energy, to her advantage. And she failed.

Though she possessed his power, the machine was in control. She knew, from the images that had coursed through his mind, that he had thought of everything. He had planned it all—down to the last detail.

And she knew she was going to die.

She also knew that, from this point forward, the process could not be stopped. She knew that if Magneto had been standing here, in her place, he wouldn't have been able to stop it, either.

A moment later, something shifted. The energy he had given her began to flow away, draining into the machine. Along with it went her own life force.

It pulled at her, painfully taking everything she had and pouring it into the spinning rings.

In the distance fireworks lit the sky.

She used to love fireworks.

She could see the beautiful colors, hear the distant explosions, as the machine pulled the blackness around her, covering her in deep and intense pain.

She fought, with one last desperate burst of energy.

But the machine took that also.

And the blackness forced her eyes closed as the pain cut at her every cell.

Then she knew she would see no more.

Magneto watched as the young girl passed out in the machine, and the rings sped up to the point where they disappeared. He had never felt so tired, so drained. Another few seconds and her touch would have killed him.

He moved out onto the observation platform facing Ellis Island, and the firework display going on there. "Give me your tired, your poor, your huddled masses," he said. Then he laughed bitterly and turned, waving at the door, willing it to close.

It didn't move.

This time he laughed at himself. Of course—it was going to take some time for his powers to return.

As his machine gained speed around Rogue, he moved to the door and closed it by hand, latching it.

A moment later the flame of the torch above him was shattered, bursting outward in an explosion that was timed to mix with the fireworks.

Perfect.

The white light started to fill the sky, joining the greens and blues and reds of the celebration.

Magneto watched in wonderment. It was almost time for the world to change.

Almost time for his world to begin.

Chapter Twenty-six

Liberty Island

Logan crouched on one spine of the statue's crown and watched as Sabretooth charged him again. Logan's claws were extended; his every sense was on full alert. He could feel his own blood pounding through his veins. It was payback time.

All he had to do was get the big guy into the air and over the edge. Gravity and the rocks below would do the rest.

But Sabretooth was too smart for that. Or he had the same damn idea.

The big mutant smashed directly into Logan, smothering him, and the two of them tumbled backward, pounding and slashing at each other as they rolled toward the tip of the metal spine.

As they came to their feet, Logan shoved himself away and slashed at his foul-smelling enemy, narrowly missing his face. But as Logan's arm came around, he realized he had snagged his own dog tags and ripped the chain off Sabretooth's neck.

"This is mine," he said, grabbing the tags and

holding them up. He stuffed them into a pocket as Sabretooth came at him again.

"You're not getting them back," Logan said.

"We'll see about that," Sabretooth said, his voice a low growl—as if that was going to rattle Logan.

The force of the attack shoved Logan back, and pinned him to the metal surface of the statue. He kicked upward, hard, catching a soft spot.

Locked again, they rolled over twice, and Sabretooth pinned Logan's arms before he could get them free. He kicked upward again, burying his knee in Sabretooth's stomach, but that didn't break the hold this time. Sabretooth lifted Logan up until he was staring directly into Sabretooth's face, held there like a small child.

Logan's hands were pinned against Sabretooth's side. He could feel Cyclops' visor tucked in a pocket. With one hand he slipped it out and shoved it up the sleeve of his new uniform.

Sabretooth was incredibly strong, and there was no way Logan could yank free. So he did the next best thing. He spit in the mutant's face.

It seemed like the right thing to do at the time.

Sabretooth laughed viciously. "That all you got?"

Logan smiled. "Nope. How about a metal skull?"

With that he smashed his forehead directly into Sabretooth's face. He could feel Sabretooth's nose break.

The grip weakened, and Logan kicked free, tumbling away.

But he wasn't fast enough.

And he was headed in slightly the wrong direction.

Sabretooth grabbed his wrist, and using Logan's

momentum, he swung him around and off the crown, into the air.

Logan spun around as he began to plummet toward the rocks below, extending his claws. Before he'd dropped more than twenty feet, he snagged one ear of the statue.

His claws dug into the metal.

One of them held.

Barely.

Yanked to a stop, he smashed into the cold metal surface.

The pain threatened to cause him to black out. He had torn his right arm out of the socket, but he didn't let go, hanging there from one claw like a bad earring.

More fireworks exploded over the water in reds and greens. Logan focused on them for a moment, letting the pain subside slightly.

The slightest wrong move and his arm would give way, or the one claw would slip from the metal. And thanks to the angle, there was nothing below him but rocks. He might live through the fall, but he wouldn't be any good for a long, long time.

Slowly, he turned his body.

The claw held.

Carefully he raised his other hand. Then, gauging exactly how much force he dared use, he stuck all four claws from his left hand into the metal of the ear, then pulled himself up a little, using the last of his strength to ease the pressure on his injured arm.

He pulled the one claw out and let the ripped-up arm drop into a natural position. He could feel the pain subside as his healing ability kicked in.

Over his head, the statue's torch exploded outward, spewing an intense white light in all directions.

Rogue!

The thought sent another burst of energy flowing into him and he climbed, hand over hand, ignoring the pain.

Ignoring the shoulder.

He had to get up there, and get up there fast.

While the fight between Logan and Sabretooth raged above, Jean had been trying to ease her way out of the metal trap, but she'd had no success at all. She was pressed tightly against a metal beam that rested between her and Cyclops, held against the metal wall of the inside of the statue's head so securely that it was hard to breathe.

"Can you see Storm?" Cyclops asked.

"Yes," she said.

Storm had been trying to slip upward, with just about as much success.

"Try mentally bending the metal away from her. Give her an inch to move."

"Ready, Storm?" Jean asked.

"The one around my chest is the tightest," Storm said. "Try it first."

Jean concentrated, using all her training to focus her attention down on the one beam. In her mind, she pictured it stretching away from Storm.

"I can feel it moving," Storm said, wiggling to move up.

Jean pushed, harder and harder.

The beam across Storm's chest was shaking, but not bending.

Finally Jean could push no farther.

"No luck," she said softly.

Cyclops nodded slightly, as much as the spikes against his temples would allow.

Overhead, the sounds of the fight stopped. Only the sounds of the distant fireworks remained. Jean held her breath, trying to sense Logan or Rogue.

She couldn't find either of them.

Suddenly Sabretooth dropped into the middle of the room with a heavy *thud*. He was bleeding in a number of places, including his nose, and his coat and furs were ripped.

There was no Logan.

That meant he had lost.

"Time to end it all," Sabretooth said. "I'll make it quick, I promise."

He walked toward Storm. Standing in front of her he raised his hand, claws out.

"No!" Jean said, focusing on his hand, freezing it in midair.

Sabretooth stared at his claws as if they were betraying him.

He stepped back, and Jean released his hand.

He turned and grinned at her. "Nice trick."

Then he stepped toward her, his hand outstretched, reaching for her neck.

"No!" she said again, even more vehemently, focusing on his hand.

Willing it to stop.

And again it froze, just a foot in front of her.

He grinned even more viciously, and pushed. He seemed to be enjoying this.

She focused with all her strength, but she knew there was no chance she could hold him back for long.

Slowly he moved forward, never losing the sick smile on his face, until finally his claws were about to touch her neck.

"Hey!" Logan said.

Sabretooth jerked around.

Jean let his hand go and gasped for breath.

She had never been so happy to see anyone in her entire life. Logan was standing there, cut in a dozen places, but healing. His new uniform looked as if it had been put through a shredder. And he was holding one shoulder a little lower than the other.

But he was alive.

He glanced at her and smiled. "What do you see?" he asked, then winked.

Suddenly she was in his mind, and she knew instantly what he wanted her to do.

"Scott," she whispered, "when I tell you, open your eyes."

"What?" Cyclops said.

"I know. Just do it and trust me."

"You'll be killed."

"No, I won't," she whispered as Sabretooth took a step toward Logan. "Now trust me."

"You know, you really smell," Logan said to Sabretooth. "And I think someone needs to change your kitty box."

Sabretooth growled a low, guttural growl, and took another step.

Logan reached into his sleeve and yanked out Cyclops' visor, then tossed it into the air.

Jean focused all her attention on the visor, snatching it out of the air and bringing it to her.

Sabretooth reacted quickly, diving for it as it shot past.

But he missed.

Jean brought the visor into position in front of Cyclops' face, snapped it open with her mind, and adjusted the control that focused the lenses.

"Now!" she said.

Cyclops opened his eyes.

The intense energy rushed into the visor. She could feel its heat, but none of it touched her.

The narrow red beam shot from the visor, went past her head and hit Sabretooth squarely in the chest, smashing him backward through the metal wall and out into the dark night sky.

"Eyes shut!" she ordered Scott. He closed his eyes, and the visor dropped to the ground as she slumped against the metal that still held her in its grip. Logan jumped to the Sabretooth-sized hole in the wall and looked down.

"Bull's-eye," he said. "Right through the roof of a boat." He turned and smiled at her. "Nice shooting."

Jean was too tired even to smile back.

"We still haven't won."

"Rogue," Logan said, moving quickly to cut them free.

"Rogue," Jean said.

As Logan cut the metal away from her and Cyclops, she could see the white light starting to spread. They had to stop Magneto, and stop him fast, or thousands were going to die just as Senator Kelly had died.

Maybe even millions, if that white energy reached Manhattan.

Chapter Twenty-seven

Ellis Island

Agent Downer couldn't even begin to identify what he was seeing coming from the torch of the Statue of Liberty. White light.

A cloud of white light.

Or a cloud of something very bright that seemed to have no substance.

Just light.

It fascinated him and scared him to death in the same instant.

He keyed his microphone. "Any contact at all with Liberty Island?"

"None."

"Rats," he said softly, glancing down at the crowds below. He had no choice.

He flipped a switch and gave the order. "Code One. Evacuate."

Below him Secret Service agents moved as a tight unit, and not far behind them the rest of the security forces jumped into action, each group taking charge of their heads of state. The president was instantly surrounded and moved quickly with the first lady toward one of the waiting cars.

Along the road that led back from Ellis Island and all the way into the city, Craig knew all traffic was being cleared. The cars were going to pour off this island far, far faster than they had come onto it. The evacuation procedures had been worked out to the last detail, practiced again and again. He just hoped it was going to be fast enough.

Across the water, the cloud of white light continued to spread.

Liberty Island

Logan finished cutting Storm loose and moved quickly to stand beside Cyclops and Jean. They were at the window, where they could see the torch above them. The white light was just as the professor had described it from the images in Senator Kelly's mind. It was pouring out of the torch and spreading toward both Ellis Island and Manhattan.

"I've got to blast it," Cyclops said.

"Not with Rogue still up there," Logan responded. He turned to Storm. "I need you to lift me up there."

"I can't control wind like that," she replied. "You could fly right over the torch."

"If I don't make it," Logan said, "then Cyclops can blast the whole damn thing." He turned to Cyclops. "You see another choice?"

Cyclops glanced up, then shook his head. "Try it."

"In the opening," Storm said, pointing to the hole Sabretooth had punched in the wall on his way out.

"Keep your body flat until you're ready to land. Then curl into a ball."

"Gotcha," Logan said.

Logan jumped up to where she had indicated, then turned. Storm's eyes had gone pure white, and the wind was starting to come up around him. Jean and Cyclops moved back against the wall and hung on while Logan stood in the opening, gripping the edge, leaning into the wind.

Suddenly he felt himself being lifted by the air, so he let go. It was like floating on a fast river of water. One moment he was in the opening; the next he was out over the bay and heading upward.

Like a parachutist, he spread his arms and legs, trying to stay flat, trying to give some surface for Storm's wind to work against.

And he was trying his best not to panic. He knew now that he really hated flying.

Above him, the torch and the white cloud of light were coming on fast.

He focused on his target. He was going to have to time this perfectly.

Just as he passed above the balcony that curved around the torch, he tucked into a tight ball, right over Magneto's head.

The look on the old mutant's face was priceless.

The wind stopped, and Logan's speed and momentum sent him shooting directly at the machine.

There was Rogue. And there were the rings, spinning.

"Oh, shoot!" he said.

Reacting instinctively, he extended his claws, and using them like a diver uses his hands to break the surface of the water, he went in.

The claws sheared through one of the rings, sending it careening off into the night air. He was moving fast enough that one of the other rings only took a nick out of one of his boots.

He hit the base of the machine and came up quickly, wrapping himself over Rogue, careful not to touch any of her bare skin, trying to protect her from any flying shards of metal.

Around him the machine continued to operate, but now it was off balance and one ring short. The entire thing started to shake as it built to full power, ripping itself apart at the same time.

Under him, Rogue jerked and twitched as the machine drained the life from her.

The white cloud of light had extended halfway to Ellis Island and was still spreading toward the city. He had to do something to stop it.

And to save Rogue.

Keeping her sheltered as best he could, he reached out with his claws and thrust them into the blur of rings that spun around him.

It was like sticking a finger into a high-speed fan.

Snap! His hand was smashed sideways as his claws sliced through another ring. Once again, his shoulder was wrenched out of its socket. New pain coursed through him, making him shout out in agony.

Now the machine around him was really tearing itself apart. The sound had changed from a humming into a massive roar, like a jet engine straining to shove a plane into the air.

Only this was one very sick engine.

The shaking was like being inside a giant blender. It was everything he could do just to hold on.

The remaining rings had lost all semblance of balance. Logan hoped fervently that the entire arm of the statue didn't fall off. It hadn't been designed to take anything like this, he was sure.

Then everything exploded around him.

The remaining rings on the massive machine tangled with a shriek of ripping and tearing metal. Then they blew outward, sending deadly fragments flashing across the bay. The air was filled with massive explosions, far louder than the fireworks had been.

The white light stalled, then just seemed to vanish. Soon it was as if it had never been there.

Logan's ears were ringing, and his arms and hands hurt from holding on so tightly. He was cut in a dozen more places, and he doubted his shoulder was ever going to be the same.

But he was alive.

And the light had been stopped.

He climbed out of the wreckage and stepped to the balcony level. Nothing much was left of the torch of Lady Liberty.

Magneto stood there, his face crimson with anger and bleeding from a gash along his forehead. He stormed toward Logan. "You have ruined it!"

"That was the plan," Logan said, bracing himself. "Just not yours."

Magneto waved his arm, and a few small pieces of wreckage went flying at Logan. But nothing big.

"Feeling a little weak, huh?" Logan asked. He batted the small hunks of metal aside like annoying flies and stepped right up into the face of the old mutant.

"You just disgust me."

Magneto's eyes went round, as if he were suddenly

very afraid for his own life. And that disgusted Logan even more.

With one hand he gripped the old man's vest and lifted him in the air. Then he extended the claws on the other hand and reared back, holding his fist up in front of Magneto's face, clearly ready to swing.

"Say good-bye," Logan growled, his voice low and mean.

Then, just as he was about to run the man through, he retracted his claws and just decked the guy with the hardest punch he could throw.

Magneto's head jerked around, his helmet flying off into space. The old mutant slumped to the surface of the statue, out cold.

Logan stood over him for a second, then shook his head. "That's a lot less than you deserve."

With a hard kick to Magneto's side for good measure, Logan turned and moved back toward Rogue.

"Come on, kid," Logan said as he dug her out of the wreckage. "Time to go home."

Suddenly he realized that she wasn't moving.

She wasn't breathing.

She was gone, still strapped into the remains of Magneto's machine.

"Oh, God, no," he said.

He cut off the metal straps and let her slump into his lap.

She didn't move.

How could this have happened?

How could he have failed?

He stared at her, then down at his own body. He was bleeding in a dozen places, and even with his regenerative powers, it was going to take him some time to heal. But that didn't matter.

He looked out at the police boats streaming toward him from Ellis Island and from the city. And at the ring of helicopters hovering close around the island, waiting for the ground forces to get into position. There wasn't much time.

Then he looked back into the face of young Rogue. She didn't deserve to die like this. He had promised her he'd take care of her. And he had failed.

He took a deep breath. Storm floated up on a wind and landed on the platform next to Magneto's body.

Maybe, just maybe, he hadn't failed yet. Maybe there was enough left for one of them.

He pulled off his gloves, reached down, and took Rogue's face in his hands.

The shock jolted him, and he could feel his energy flowing into her.

On his chest, his wounds reopened, and his bleeding started to get much worse.

With his hands still holding the soft skin of her face, the blackness took him.

Chapter
Twenty-eight

Liberty Island

Agent Downer climbed the last few stairs into the torn head of the Statue of Liberty. The evacuation of Ellis Island had gone fairly smoothly, all things considered, and now Liberty Island was also secure. What had happened here was going to take some time to figure out, if anyone would ever really know.

He had almost forty of New York's finest dead, and a national treasure had been trashed. The only clue at all as to what had happened was a machine that lay in ruins where the statue's torch used to be.

And an unconscious man.

Craig moved to the center of the room and stared down at the man. No one had touched him. Not until he got there. Those had been his orders.

He knelt down, being careful to not touch anything.

A hypo lay on the floor beside him.

Craig straightened up and took a deep breath, looking around. Hunks of metal lay everywhere. Some had been bent like noodles; others were sliced like cheese.

It would take a lot of talking to pin all this death and

destruction on one man. He shook his head. It was a strange new world they were all living in, that was for sure. And things like this wouldn't make his job any easier.

"Get him into a holding cell," Craig ordered the men standing nearby. "And for God's sake, don't let him wake up until we get him into the right kind of place."

Craig moved over to the window and looked across at Ellis Island. They had come very close tonight to a disaster, that much he did not doubt. That white cloud would have reached most of the world's leaders before the evacuation could have been completed.

What the white cloud would have done to them was unknown, but Craig doubted it would have been anything good.

But who had saved them?

Who had saved the world tonight?

Someday, he hoped to know the answer to that question.

X-Men Mansion

The blackness seemed to swim, then it began taking on form, taking on shapes.

He organized the shapes, pushed the blackness into patterns, then searched for the light.

"This way, Professor," a familiar voice said.

So he moved that way, organizing, shaping as he went.

"This way," the voice said again.

He followed.

And after what seemed like a short time, in a place

where time didn't seem relevant at all, Professor Xavier saw a dot of light in the far distance.

"That's right," the voice said. "Go to the light."

The light grew as he focused on it, until finally it surrounded him, flooding into his mind, his conscious thoughts. So he opened his eyes.

"Welcome back," Jean said, smiling down at him.

Xavier let himself smile. He felt surprisingly refreshed, almost as if waking from a long nap.

"I knew you could make it," Jean said.

"I had a good guide," he answered, taking her hand and squeezing it. Then he remembered what had been going on when he went into Cerebro.

He looked up at her. "What happened?"

"We stopped Magneto," Jean said, smiling. She stepped aside and looked over her shoulder. The professor could see Logan on the table across the lab, tubes running from his arms. "He's not healing," Jean said softly.

The professor nodded, then took a deep breath. "I think I have some catching up to do."

"And resting," Jean said.

"That, I've been doing," he said. "I think I have enough energy for a story before my next nap."

She laughed softly, wistfully, and pulled up a chair.

An hour later he knew it all.

An hour later he was prouder of his students than he ever could have imagined being.

Logan's nightmare kept him, held him, like the straps holding him to the table.

The same events, over and over.

Strapped down, his skeleton drawn on his skin.

Lowered into the vat of fluid.

Scalpels cutting at him, over and over.

The pain.

Intense pain.

And then it would start again.

Until finally it changed.

As they lowered him into the vat, he tried to fight back, just as he always did, to attack those around him, even though he was tied down.

But a strong voice said, "Logan."

A friendly voice.

A firm voice.

Logan looked up into the face of Professor Xavier.

"Logan, tell me what happened to you."

So instead of being cut on this time, he broke the cycle.

Logan told the professor as much as he could, walking him through the nightmare like a guide.

And for the first time, he didn't feel the pain.

Jean sat with Cyclops, Storm, and about two dozen of the older students in the large recreational room, staring at the large-screen television. Outside the weather was beautiful, the sun shining in the big windows, warming the space. Yet all of them, Jean included, were ignoring the weather for the moment. Instead they were watching the news. She knew that their entire future, maybe the world's future, rested in no small part on what was happening today in the Senate.

"Quiet now," Storm said to the kids as the anchorman came back on.

"Even after last week's terrorist attack on the Statue

of Liberty by suspected mutants, the outcome of the Senate vote just moments ago was fifty against, forty-nine in favor of the Mutant Registration Act. It has been defeated."

Jean felt as if her heart were about to explode out of her chest.

Around her the children shouted and cheered and stamped their feet, hugging and even crying.

She thought she might cry, too, the relief was so great. She couldn't believe the bill had been defeated. After what had happened at the Statue of Liberty, she had just assumed it would pass.

"Quiet!" Cyclops ordered. "Everybody quiet!"

The anchorman continued with his report. "Many feel that this narrow defeat was due, in large part, to the disappearance of Senator Robert Kelly, who until this last week, provided the loudest voice in the cry for mutant registration. No sign of Senator Kelly has yet been found. Police fear foul play."

Jean stood, wiping her hands on her pants as if that would finally clean off the entire distasteful subject of mutant registration. She wished it would, but she knew, as did everyone in the room, that the attempt to control mutants was far from over.

With a glance at Rogue, standing near the window, Jean left the talking and cheering group and headed down to the medical lab. Rogue had come through everything just fine; the only outward sign of her ordeal was a streak of white hair.

But Logan wasn't faring as well.

A minute later she was beside Logan's bed in the medical lab. Having had a few sessions with the professor, he seemed to be resting easier.

She uncapped a new IV and started to put it into Logan's arm.

Suddenly, just as had happened the first time she had treated him, Logan raised his hand up and grabbed her. But this time his touch was gentle, and he grasped her arm instead of her neck.

"Hey," he said, opening his eyes to look at her.

"Hey, yourself," she said, smiling down at him. "How are you feeling?"

"Fantastic," he lied.

She laughed. Clearly he was in deep pain. But it was just like him to say he was fine.

She checked under one bandage on his arm. His wound was healing now, and healing quickly. It looked as if he was coming back.

"That was a brave thing you did for Rogue," she said as she replaced his bandage.

"Did it work?" he asked.

"She's fine," Jean said, holding his hand. "She took on a few of your more charming personality traits for a few days, but we lived through it."

Jean leaned in close and whispered. "I think she's a little taken with you."

"Well," he said, smiling, "you can tell her my heart belongs to someone else."

Jean stared at him. There was no doubt the two of them shared a unique connection. And she admired him a great deal. But her love was with Scott.

"You know," she said, "you and I—"

Logan smiled. "How's Xavier doing?"

She laughed. He had let her off the hook.

"He's good."

"Good," Logan said, and Jean could tell he actually meant it. Then he closed his eyes.

A moment later he was snoring.

Chapter
Twenty-nine

X-Men Mansion

Professor Xavier rolled his chair up and activated the holographic map table as Logan watched, still amazed at the gadget. The images of rugged, tree-covered mountain ranges appeared. Logan could see the roads, the streams, the old fire burns. Every damned detail of the area.

Flatout amazing.

The two of them were alone in the big room, so Logan moved over to a position beside the professor, standing over the display.

Using the controls on the side of the machine, Xavier focused down on a high pass, and Logan followed the focus, feeling as if he knew the area, yet not remembering it at all.

"There is an abandoned military compound at Alkali Lake, in the Canadian Rocky Mountains," Xavier said, pointing at the pass and a small lake that sat a distance off the main road. "It's not far from where we found you. There's not much left of it, but you may find some answers."

Logan studied it for a moment, logging it all in his

memory. Then he looked over at the professor. "Thank you."

It seemed like such a small thing to say for what the professor had done for him. But at the moment it was just going to have to be enough.

"You're welcome," Xavier said, flicking the map off and rolling away from the now-empty table. "You know there's always a place for you here."

"I know," Logan said.

Jean and Scott and Storm had also made that very clear. And for the first time since he had woken up in that meadow, his only memories being nightmares of pain, he felt as if he had a place to go—a place he almost belonged. This mansion was now his home. It was a wonderful feeling.

"Are you going to say good-bye to the rest?" Xavier asked.

"No," Logan said. Then he smiled. "I suspect they already know I'm going for a little trip."

Xavier laughed, a twinkle in his eye. "I suspect you may be right about that."

Logan moved to stand in front of the professor and extended his hand. "I'll be seeing you."

Xavier shook the hand, holding it tightly, then nodded. "Good luck."

Ten minutes later Logan was headed down the front steps of the mansion, toward the driveway. The professor had said there would be transportation waiting there for him to use. What he found was Cyclops' wonderful black motorcycle, the same one Logan had stolen to get to the train station.

The keys were in the ignition, and there was a note taped to the gas tank. *Good luck. Scott.*

He laughed and kicked the motorcycle to life. If he couldn't say anything else for old Visor Boy, he had good taste in women and motorcycles. And he was a pretty fine leader to boot.

Logan sat on the bike, letting the smooth rumble of the engine surround him for a moment. The day was gorgeous—not too hot, not too cold. Perfect weather to start a trip.

Without even a look back, he headed down the driveway. He knew he'd be seeing the place again.

On the big front lawn a bunch of the students were playing soccer, Rogue among them. He pulled over and stopped, letting the engine idle as he watched her run and play and laugh, being what seemed like a normal kid.

She deserved that much at least, while she still had some childhood left.

After a moment she looked up and saw him. With a wave she ran his way, smiling, looking happy and flushed from the exercise. He put out a gloved hand and took hers.

She nodded, seemed about to say something, then let go of his hand and looked down into her palm. He'd given her his dog tags.

She stared at them for a moment, then looked up at him, tears appearing in her eyes. "Thank you."

"No," he said, smiling. "Thank you."

She had no idea what she had done for him. Maybe, ten years from now, she would understand. They'd talk about it. Maybe.

With that, he straightened his back, clicked the engine into gear, and with a smile for Rogue, headed down the driveway. He had some of his past to find, some answers to dig out of some ruins in the Canadian Rocky Mountains.

Then he could come home.

Now he had a future.

Epilog

Xavier smiled across the chess table at his old friend, Eric. They hadn't played chess in years, and Xavier hadn't realized how much he'd missed it until now. Maybe they would have to make this a regular occurrence. Maybe.

Xavier moved a pawn.

Eric nodded. "Doesn't it ever wake you in the middle of the night, the feeling that someday, someday very soon, they will pass that foolish law?"

He also moved a pawn to counter Charles' move, then kept talking. "Or maybe a law like it. And they will come for you and your children, and take you all away."

"It bothers me very much indeed, Eric," Xavier said, moving a knight.

"And what will you do when you wake up to that happening?" Eric asked. He moved a rook two spaces forward.

"I will feel a great swell of pity," Xavier said, "for the poor soul who comes to that school looking for trouble."

He made a pawn move; Eric countered with another rook.

"You know this is war, don't you, Charles?"

Xavier nodded. The board was beginning to look like a one-sided war, as well. He had all his pieces in position, and it didn't even seem as if Eric had noticed.

"And I intend to fight this war by any means necessary," Eric continued. He aggressively moved a knight, again ignoring what Xavier was doing.

"And I will always be there, old friend," Xavier said. With that he moved his queen two spaces, taking away one of Eric's knights.

"Check," he said. He didn't add the word "mate." There was no need.

He pushed his plastic wheelchair back from the board and smiled at his old friend. "Thanks for the game, Eric."

Then he turned to the clear plastic door. Beyond that were nothing but plastic walls. There wasn't an ounce of metal within a half mile of this cell. It was a very special jail, designed for one very special occupant.

"Why do you come here, Charles?" Eric asked as Xavier reached the door and the guard on the other side opened it.

Xavier looked back. "Why do you ask me questions to which you already know the answers?"

"Ah, yes," Eric said, smiling. "I forgot about your continuing search for hope."

The two looked at each other for a moment. Then Eric said, "It could be our world, Charles."

"It's always been our world, Eric. It's only when we lose sight of that that we imprison ourselves."

He wheeled out, and the plastic door slid shut behind him. His old friend was left studying the board. And wondering what he had done wrong.

About the Authors

DEAN WESLEY SMITH was a founder of the well-respected small press Pulphouse. He has written a number of novels—both his own and as tie-in projects—including *Laying the Music to Rest* and *X-Men: The Jewels of Cyttorak*.

KRISTINE KATHRYN RUSCH is the Hugo and World Fantasy Award–winning former editor of *The Magazine of Fantasy and Science Fiction*. She turned to writing full-time two years ago. She, too, has written a number of original and tie-in novels, including the *Fey* series and *Star Wars: The New Rebellion*.

Explore the X-MEN Universe Online!!!

For uncanny content and shopping visit

www.marvel.com/x-men
and
www.toysrus.com/xmen